David J Davis

Ddavis9.dd96@gmail.com

The Night the stone fell

by

David J Davis

Table of Contents

Chapter 1

Life in the valley

In a small town of about one thousand people sits a valley below a huge mountain. Now their homes or down in the valley but the mountain is full of giant rocks. Which they have tried to have removed, but the local government, says it could cause a catastrophic rockslide; in the dry season there was nothing to worry about. Except maybe a Ram knocking over one of the stones trying to escape from the mountain lions. Yes, they lived in an unsafe neighborhood. But they lived incredibly happy and dedicated lives. Most were coal miners that mined the nearby, mountains. But Tommy and Sarah were the local game wardens and served as the marshals of the town. They dealt with poachers and kids most of the time. Occasionally there would be a murder to investigate. The town had an old drive in theater that the teens frequented a lot. They did manage to keep up with the latest movie. Sarah would frequently monitor the mountains and the stability of the stones. One day as she was walking through the mountain's forest line. She happens upon a mountain lion. Which she immediately notices and springs into action pulling her firearm out of its holster. The mountain lion charges and jumps Sarah fires! She winds up flat on her back on the ground. With the mountain lion on top of her! She removes the dead animal from off her chest, his mouth lunged at her throat. "You, will make a fine throw rug, there kitty" she speaks to the dead animal as she drags the cat back and puts it on a lift made of hydraulic parts and lifts the cat into the back of her truck. She radios "Coming in

Mountain secure" she says to dispatch. She leaves out the part about the cougar. She did not want to upset the animal lovers too much. She loved them too, but she was not about to allow that big cat to kill her!

She arrives back at the station and motions for Tommy to come here. Tommy walks over to Sarah. "What is it, what you got there?" Tommy says jokingly but then jumps once he sees the dead animal staring at him. "Where you see him?" Tommy asked. "Near the base of the mountain, I was nearly home when I was attacked." Sarah responds. "Strange, I never noticed them, being this far down the valley before." Tommy comments. "How were the Stones up there?" Tommy asked. "They are seemingly okay" Sarah says. The valley was surrounded by these huge stones that were shaken loose by a major Earthquake several years ago. They shook several of the stones loose and they rolled to a stop about three hundred feet above the village. So, every year they must monitor the security of the stones. For when the stones came to a stop before, they put up fences to keep them in place. But every time an Earthquake hits, they must sure up the rocks; so, they would not fall onto, the town. A town over had this happen and they are no longer there. It is just a pile of rubble. Thousands of people lie buried deep under the layer of rocks in a rocky grave. Of course, we do not want that to happen to us, so we, have put up huge fences; to keep them in check. We had one fall last year and it leveled three fourths of the road. We are still trying to rebuild the road; it could take up to six months. To repair the bridge, we had to get rid of the boulder. Now! You must be thinking why in the world would you live in something like this. My answer is this: you, would have to see it for yourself. The majestic mountains overlooking the valleys far and wide. Wildlife of all kinds including mountain lions and timber wolves. Even wolverines and bears have been seen here. The hiking is great, the fishing is like none other; the deer out here look like Clydesdale horses. They are so big and tall; they are a hunter's dream come true. Were in a whole different part of the world, there are no cell towers, Wi-Fi or internet hot spots here. But

6

there are is an internet connection. If you, want coffees and conversation? Then come on down to miss Bell's, she has the best coffee in town. Come to think of it, she is the only one in town. Everybody knows everybody, and nothing happens without Miss Linda Lou, finding out about it. After all she is the town gossip and the local sheriff's secretary for the police station. Life here is a lot slower than in the big cities. If you, do not like quiet and relaxing do not come here you, will be miserable. Nothing to do around here but fish, hunt and play musical instruments and sing. We have a blue grass barn in which talent from all over comes to play. Well, thanks for stopping by! Tommy says as he finishes talking to the couple that came to visit. They were looking for a honeymoon spot as they were to marry in the spring. Tommy walks the couple to their car. Come back anytime and thanks for stopping by. Tommy said with his country twang accent. Later that day a band of motorcyclists came riding through. They were preparing for the Olympics that were to be held near there. Overall a rather peaceful day Tommy closes the police station and locks the door, Sarah is already home and has supper already for Tommy and her to eat. After dinner they both do the dishes and have some conversations. "So, you, killed a mountain lion? "Tommy asked with a smirk on his face. The night waxes late they go to bed. The next morning would be more of the same as yesterday except there would be a minor earthquake. It was about 9am when the tremors began it was a bad one. Plates fall and crash to the floor a sign falls from its post and crashes to the ground. After the violent shaking all returned to normal. But the damage had already been done. Trees lay in the road signs lay on the ground. A couple of homes had been flattened. Mr. Jones' house had caved in killing him with falling lumber. Life in the valley was relaxing and nice. But there were real dangers here that could take your life. It took them a couple of weeks to clean everything up. Once they did, they were able to go back to life as normal.

Chapter 2

A day of unrest

After the minor quake things seemed to be okay. The canceled festival would be rescheduled. Life

would go on but would it? Living amongst nature can be extremely rewarding; but also, extremely

dangerous. A group of kids were going on a field trip from the city to the valley. They would be there

in an hour. While they were on their way up, Tommy and Sarah were getting things ready by putting

up barriers and mapping off safer less inhabited trails. On the bus the Teacher was giving instruction

to her fourth-grade class. "Don't veer off the paths and stay close to your buddy" Samantha the

teacher said. They would stop four times for bathroom breaks. Upon arriving Samantha instructs

them to slowly get off the bus and make a line. A straight line! Five minutes later Tommy and Sarah have greeted them and brought them to the beautiful trail heads. The more rewarding but more dangerous trails were blocked off. They start down the road and a few of the kids take off. Tommy goes after them but before he could get there, he hears a scream! The kids had stumbled on a porcupine and one of them had gotten stuck with some of the needles. "It's too dangerous to run off by yourself boys. Understand?" Tommy asks. "Yes, sir we, know now, we won't do it again." Tommy believed them but keeps them close as they airlift the young boy back to the hospital. The hike continues: as a mountain lion wonders in front of them, "What is he doing down here?" Tommy wondered. The children gasped some cried. Tommy fires his pistol in the air and the lion runs off. They get to a rest area Tommy and Sarah talk. That lion never comes this far down it must be running out of food up there. Better have Harvey check it out up there. Sarah grabs her walkie and calls officer Harvey. "Harvey can you check out the mountain we saw a cougar down here," "Sure thing Sarah." Harvey responds. "Thanks Harvey." "your welcome" Harvey signs out and heads up the mountain. As he approaches, he notices a lot of dead flowers and animals, as he got closer, he smelled a foul order. Harvey hollers gas! And gets on the radio! Get them kids out of here! There is a major gas leak one spark and boom. I am calling the gas company! "He drives to safe area as Tommy grabs a little girl and takes off, they all start running. As they all get to safety smoke rises from a lightning strike. A fire! Everybody ducks everyone hits the floor! A loud bang! Then a huge fireball shoots in the air and dissipates. The ground shakes trees fall a power pole falls destroying the bus. The kids clap and scream, then laugh. Then they cry because they cannot go home. After the smoke settles the bus is completely damaged. There would be no getting it back on the road! Now, the teachers, kids and bus driver were stuck there. With no way of getting in touch with anyone else to get them back. The communications had been wiped out due to the explosion. Also, Harvey was missing too. Tommy tries to reach him on his radio, but no answer. It was a total mess trees on the road, smoke everywhere. It seemed like a warzone. The kids were crying and going crazy. Sarah calms them down and moves them in to the Courthouse waiting area. It was the safest place for them, until they could find Harvey. They needed to restore communications, get these kids back home and clean up this mess. First, they head back to the spot where Harvey had first warned them. Look! Sarah screams to Tommy as he was a good distance away. What it is? Tommy shouted back. Sarah holds up Harvey's radio that had been crushed, it appeared to have been dropped on these rocks she said. Let us keep looking then. They walk a little way to a ditch just off the road. Help! Did you hear that Sarah asked? Hear what? Help! That she said. Tommy walks to the edge to see where it was coming from. He looks in the ditch and hanging upside down by his feet from a tree was Harvey! Hang in there Harvey! Tommy laughs as he said it. Very funny Harvey smirks. Tommy climbs down and grabs Harvey while Sarah had climbed and loosened his feet. Harvey a young man average height and weight falls headfirst into Tommy's arms. Gotcha! Tommy says as he gently lets him down. What happened Harvey? I was patrolling the area and smelled gas, there was a campfire nearby and before I could act. Boom! The gas ignited throwing me in this ditch. Campfire? You said? Yes, it was a small campfire and a tent. Oh my, we need to see if anyone was there!

Harvey, Sarah, and Tommy run to the spot where the explosion happened. It was a charred area of blackness and smoky area with embers of fire still burning and sizzling on the ground. They find the tent, or what was left of it. There was no sign of anyone yet, but they kept looking, Sarah screams in horror! Harvey and Tommy run to see what was wrong. When they arrive, three burnt bodies lie next to each other. A father, mother and child. They never knew what hit them they were killed when the gas ignited. The flame was so hot it just burnt them to a crisp. Wonder who they were? And better yet when did they arrive? All campers were to register with the station before camping, but there was no record of anyone camping out here currently. We will need to investigate this further but first we need to restore communications and get those kids home. The three of them head up the mountain to the cell tower. They notice the tower had fallen and wires were snapped. It will take some time to get this fixed Harvey says. Harvey a former communications expert for the military knew how to fix it. I just need the tools from the office. I will run get them Sarah says. As she leaves Tommy and Harvey to work on the tower. They clear the rubble from the tower and begin to search for any further damages. They walk into the communications shed I can patch into the town police through Morse coding with this keyboard device. Harvey begins typing in the codes. The town police may or may not see it in time, there true hope lied in getting that tower fixed. About this time Sarah comes back in the truck with the tools. How are the Kids holding up? Tommy asked Sarah. There getting antsy but there hanging in there. She replied. That is good we will see if we can get them home before nightfall, then. Harvey grabs his tools. With some wire, cutters and a hammer he begins repairing the tower. That should do it! Harvey says. Now, let us get it back up there and get those kids home. The three of them grab the tower and heave onto the winch and liftin device they crank the dial raising it up into place. Harvey begins reattaching the wires. Got it! He exclaims as he runs inside and begins to turn on the computer. With a few taps here and there the communications were restored, this is the valley police department come in. Hello, Captain Steven's here to whom am I speaking? Captain Stevens this Is Marshall Tommy Fulton. Oh, hey Tommy longtime no talk.

What can I do for you Marshall? We have about 40 fourth graders, a Teacher named Samantha and an injured bus driver that all need a ride home. Plus, one of the kids is at county general being treated for porcupine needles. Goodness what on Earth happened out there? Steven's asked. We had a gas explosion that leveled the bus and few other things, as well as killing a family of three yet to be identified. They were camping near the lake. Good grief Tommy that is terrible. We will get a bus up there right away it should be there in an hour. Thanks Captain. Call me Jim. I will need your help Jim with this family. But first let us get these kids home and get some rest. I will be in touch. Alright Tommy you have my number let me know what I can do. Will do JIM have a good one. I will have Harvey let you know when the bus arrives. It was around 1pm when the kids arrive it was now 6pm and the bus finally arrives. They load the kids the Teacher and the driver. Samantha the teacher says goodbye to Harvey as she slips him her number. They had been talking and had hit it off. Harvey says he will call and the bus cranks and rolls away. A busy day of unrest and excitement. Just an average day here in the mountain valley town.

Chapter 2

A night with no end!

Tommy and Sarah, head back to the station with Harvey. They get in their truck and say goodbye to Harvey who stayed at the station for a while longer. Tommy and Sarah arrive at their three-bedroom cabin style home. They open the door walk in and close the door walk to the bedroom and fall on the bed fast asleep they were so tired. About three hours into the night. Around

10pm Tommy is awakened to loud knocking on his door. Tommy runs to the door It was Harvey! He

was covered in blood not his own and was dripping wet from the pouring rain. Harvey! What? Before

Tommy could finish Harvey fell down weeping and wailing! What is it? Tommy insisted. Harvey

gathers himself. A tree fell onto Linda Lou's house striking her husband in the head. He was in bad

shape she called me I tried to stop the bleeding but was unsuccessful. He bled to death in my arms.

Linda Lou is tore up and I do not know what to do. We will need to call the morgue in the morning

put a cloth over his body and send Linda to her sister's. We will get a hold of the authorities and the

insurance in the morning. Harvey nodded already did this. Harvey began crying again. What is it

boy? Tell me what is wrong. Well, the explosion did not just kill that family! It busted the protection

border, about an hour ago three of them rocks fell into the courthouse killing Judge Matthews and

destroying the courthouse anything else? The bus that left with the kids was knocked off the road

and no one knows where it was and where it is now. Alright, let us get a search party and a

helicopter, call the town police and let them know. Harvey picks up the radio Tommy begins calling

the volunteer militia group. Sarah sleepy eyed comes in. What's wrong Tommy? The bus has

wrecked, and we do not know where the children are. Oh, no! Sarah grabs her flashlight, coat, gun

and keys. Let us go! She says. Tommy throws on his coat as they were still in their uniforms. They

get in the truck with Harvey in back with a big spotlight. They head south in the direction the bus

had went miles of dirt and debris lay on the road. What happened Sarah asked. Harvey said that the

explosion had broken the barrier and sent three stones that crashed the town and highway. Anyone

killed? Yes, Judge Matthews in the courthouse. Linda Lou's husband James died when a tree fell into their home. Oh, my! How's Linda? She is in shock Harvey sent her to her sister's home. Julie will be a

comfort to Linda. Sarah said. I am concerned for Harvey James bled out in his arms. He came to our

house soaked in his blood and was a mess. I just pray the children are okay and that teacher

Samantha and those drivers are okay, I know Harvey likes her a lot. Tommy commented.

As we grew closer to where we believed the bus to be, we drove slower and rolled down the windows,

Harvey yelling on the megaphone. Calling out to them, to Samantha all the while shining the light in any

direction the faintest sound would come. We drove for what seemed about three hours, when we hear a

faint voice in the distance. Stop the car! Harvey exclaimed as he shined the light down an embankment.

There were skid marks and a violent disruption of the side of the road. This had to be the place! Harvey hops

down and skids down the embankment. It is not the bus Harvey yells with a bit a disappointment in his voice.

What is it? Tommy asks as he shined down his light. It is a Jeep! Anyone in it? Nope, the driver is missing.

Come back up then! Wait! What is it? I hear something. Harvey disappears into the darkness. Harvey shines

his flashlight calling out. Anybody there? After a few minutes there is a few cries of children in the distance.

Got something. Harvey radios Tommy. Coming to you hang on. 10/4 Harvey agrees and a few minutes later

Tommy and Sarah came rolling up in the truck. What have you got? I heard some children crying a few

hundred feet up that way. He points as he jumps in the back. They drove down the road for few minutes they

spot the bus laying on its side upon closer observation. One of the drivers was pinned under the bus and the

bus was near a cliff with a 30-foot drop. The kids along with Samantha were on the bus and the bus was

teething on the edge, one wrong move and the bus and the kids and Samantha would go down the side of

the Clift. About this time the Helicopter arrives. The voice from the chopper calls out. We will lower some

cables, attach them to the axles and the frame of the bus. We will act as an anchor while you direct the children off the bus. We attach the cables, the driver that was pinned had died so we signal the chopper; it begins to pull the bus back upright and away from the cliff. As soon as the bus uprights itself we begin offloading the kids. One by one they all get off Including Samantha who jumped into Harvey's arms and kissed him. Realizing what she had done, she steps back and blushes. Sorry! Do not be! Harvey says with a grin. The driver of the first bus was about to get off when a minor earthquake shook the bus snapping the cords, sending them into the blades causing the chopper to lose control. Everybody come this way hurry! Tommy screams as the Chopper crashed into the bus sending it over the Clift and erupting into a great fire ball. Harvey. Samantha, Tommy and Sarah and all the kids gasp in horror. Sirens light up the sky as another chopper and three ambulances and a firetruck come running. And at 1 am another greyhound bus this time, rolls up with the parents hugging their kids weeping and thanking God. Their kids were okay, and they were taking them home. Samantha and Harvey talk, and Harvey agrees to take her home. Sarah looked at Tommy and sighs. Let us go home. finally. Tommy nods and they get in the truck to head home. As they drive the long road home, they see the damage left behind. The courthouse leveled; Linda Lou's house lay with a gaping hole in the roof. James her husband lay dead and to top it all off it began to rain very heavily. The thunder rolled and lightening flashed and the wind blew. They arrive home and run from the car to the house and shut the door. They sat on the couch and fall asleep in each other's arms. Around 4am they are awakened by rain falling on their heads. They jump up to find their roof had partly been blew off! Thank God! We were kept safe During the morning a tornado had blown over ripping part of their roof off. A knock at the door! It was Harvey he had a big ole smile. Good morning folks Harvey said. Good morning, what time is it? 9am did you guys see that Tornado? Harvey asks without seeing the hole in the roof. Tommy just points to the roof. Oh, Harley exclaims! Guess you guys went through it. Guess we did, slept through it woke up to the rain falling on our heads.

You were blessed then. Harvey said. Yes, yes, we surely were. So, what we need to do? Nothing much, already took care of everything you guys need a day off. Get some sleep. Wait! What about the coroner, the carpenters, and insurance? Yes, Yes, and Yes. What about the counseling? Got that covered Samantha and some of her friends are coming from their church and bringing some psychiatrist also. Alright then guess you have it covered then. You know where we will be then. Let us know if you need us. Will do Tommy. Got to go Samantha and her church will be here soon. Plus, the adjusters and everyone else.

Chapter 3

Terror in the town

Harvey leaves just in time to greet Samantha and her youth group of about 70. The adjusters and counselors all roll up their sleeves and begin to work. They begin removing shrapnel and rocks and other destruction that hindered the carpenters. All seemed to be going well, homes were being repaired, folks were getting much needed counsel. Linda and Julie came, and Linda got some grief counseling. Harvey had

got it all together and the town was beginning to heal. Samantha and Harvey sit on a swing porch at the

station drinking some sweet tea. How long have you been teaching? Harvey asked. Just 3 years. Got started

at the Elementary school right after graduation. Where did you get your degree? Liberty University online. I

worked as a teacher's aide while going to school. How about you? Oh, I graduated from Trinity Law school

with a bachelor's degree in law enforcement and have took classes to be a lawyer and have passed the B.A.R

so I hope to be a lawyer for Church ministries as it pertains to Christian rights. How long have you been

working as an officer? About 2years, I was in the military for 2 years before I began working for Tommy at 21.

Do you have any dreams of being anything other than a teacher? Or any other wishes? A teacher is all I ever

wanted to be I do dream of teaching in other countries from time to time. But I do enjoy cooking to help curb

some of the poverty in the third world countries, I know teaching and cooking does not solve it. But if the

children apply what they learn I think that is what will bring change. I agree, applying what we learn is the

key to making change happen in our lives. If all we did was learn, we could never change our situation. It

takes knowledge, wisdom and action to make something happen. Do you have any brothers, sisters? I have

two brothers, Billy and Charlie. How about you Harvey? I have one sister I have not spoken to or seen in over

a year. Her name is Nicole. Sorry to hear that. Do not be, she and I are close; she just is stationed somewhere

in the Middle East. No one can know where she is or what she is doing. OH, secret military? Yeah, she is a

Navy Seal. Wow! Our family are all military. I was a radio operator for the tanks. Sounds exciting. It was, but

not nearly as exciting as living here. Harvey grins. Samantha chuckles. Guess we better get back to work

then, Yep, but before we do. Yes? Would you come to church with me Sunday? Samantha asks as she gives

him those flirty eyes. Sure, thing when and what time? 10am at this address. Samantha hands him the address with a kiss on the cheek as she walked away. Harvey blushes and looks at the note: 3421 Riverside

Drive, Faith Baptist Church. Harvey folds the bulletin and puts it away in his wallet. As he goes to survey the

progress. A roaring sound could be heard in the distance. The roaring got closer and louder as it got closer,

they could see a semi barreling down the mountain! Not slowing, only gaining speed. The truck would be in

town in minutes. If he did not stop it, it would crash right into the crowd of folks killing some and destroying

property and possibly damaging the courthouse they had begun to repair. Harvey springs into action! He

quickly hops in a nearby bulldozer and parks it sideways and then grabs everything he could. Others jump in

grabbing cement barriers and driving other tractors in its path. Everyone get behind the courthouse! Harvey

yells as they head that way the truck smashes into the barriers and capsizes. As it does Harvey sees it is a

Hazardous chemical tanker. Everyone get down! Cover your mouth and nose with something. As the truck

skids to a stop sparks flying and the fluid inside leaking out onto the ground. The sparks hit the fluid and

Boom! A humongous explosion that rocked the town, setting off car alarms, house alarms and setting off

chain explosions. It looked like the fourth of July fireworks across America all in one place! Windows

shattered it was a nightmare! The sirens and smoke shook Tommy awake! What on Earth? He grabs his

radio. Harvey! Come in Harvey! No answer. Tommy jumps to his feet and throws on his clothes and runs to

the door, Sarah cries out! Tommy? Yes, dear? What is going on? I am not sure I felt a jarring and it woke me. I

tried Harvey, but no answer. Go, see what is happened. I will be out there in a minute. Tommy sticks his head

out the door. A plume of smoke rises in the air. Sirens and dogs howling cats meowing it seemed as a scene

out of a Bruce Willis, Die Hard movie. It was awful Tommy walked the street. It was quiet as he got to the

Courthouse. As he approached Harvey steps out. Tommy! Harvey shouts with Samantha in hand. Then the

rest of the crowd emerges. What on EARTH? A truck came flying off the mountain and slammed into our barriers, that we happened to make just in time. A runaway truck? Yes, I did not hear anything on the radio or had no warning until I heard the roaring of the engine. You did good Harvey no one was hurt, and you saved most of the town from further damage. I also see you have made progress on the courthouse. Good job thanks for giving us time to rest. Let us see if we can get this mess cleaned up! I already called hazmat and they are coming. Good, we need to see why this truck rammed our town and what happened to the driver. So, first let us get these fine folk home. I will give you some time to do this, seeing as how you and Samantha are sweet on each other and all. Harvey grins and nods and walks toward the bus. Samantha calls for her group they walk over and load up. Harvey and Samantha talk. See you Sunday then? Yes, sure thing. Enjoyed talking with you and glad you guys came and are all safe. We are thanks to God and you Harvey she says as she reaches and gives him a kiss. The youth make a bunch of funny noises to embarrass her and him she blushes, and he blushes. She hops on the bus and he steps away, as he watches them drive off. Harvey come here. Tommy calls out. Coming. Harvey says as he skips along. What is it? He asks Tommy. Tommy grins. First wipe off that pink lipstick and then we can talk. Harvey blushes and wipes his mouth on his sleeve. That is better, now look at this. What is it? It was a remote device. You mean? Yeah, I mean, someone remote drove this into town. But why? Harvey wondered. I am not sure, but we are going to get to the bottom of this. First, we need to find out who that family was! The ones who got killed at the first explosion. We were able to scrape some DNA off their charred bodies, we sent it to Denver for analysis we should find out who they were. Maybe this might begin to unravel this mystery. I sent it off right after we found them. They should be getting back with me soon. Follow up on that Harvey. As soon as we can get a name, we can get some answers I feel all this may have to do with that family.

Chapter 4

The investigation

Later that morning Sarah came to Tommy. What happened? Someone tried to take out our town. With a

remote-controlled Hazardous semi driving straight into town. Why would anyone want to destroy or harm

anyone or anything in this town? Sarah questioned. I do not know but You, Harvey and I are going to find out

the answer to these questions. This is a serious crime, an act of terrorism. Where do we begin? First Harvey is

finding out the results of the DNA of our burnt family. Second, we are going to contact Captain Stevens and

have this remote device analyzed. Once we find the answers to these questions, we shall get to the bottom

of this mystery. What do you need me to do? Sarah asked. I need you to interview some of the locals and the

business owners. We need to see if there is any connection that might give us a motive or suspect. I will get right on it. Sarah walks away and grabs her phone. I just heard from the Lab! Harvey says back at the station.

Okay tell me, who were they? The man was a wildlife photographer, the wife was a D.A. For the Miami

Courts. The kid, a girl was in middle school in Jacksonville Elementary. Their names? All I could get was the

Thompson family. Their names were sealed. Sealed? Yes, I believe they were in witness protection. This

would explain the first explosion. But not the other attacks. No, but it is better than what we had. True, what

did you get from Stevenson. Not much, just a list of possible locations and origins. Such as? Harvey inquiries.

Well, first it could be from a remote-controlled vehicle, or could be from a drone based remote sensors.

Other sources say that it could be a computer program that is used to program remote tanks. All of which

leaves us too broad of a span to ever find the true source. However, Steven has said about 200 miles north of

here, there is a drone manufacturing plant. Up for a road trip? Sure, how long will this take? It was Friday

afternoon and he was to call Samantha at 7pm. It should not take more than three hours. Want me to get

Sarah, instead? No, I can go just want to be able to call Samantha by 7. You will be fine you can pause and

call her if you need to then, Alright then let us go! Meet you at the Truck Harvey, got to let Sarah know.

Harvey heads over to the truck while Tommy radios Sarah. Sarah come in Sarah. Yes, Tommy? Harvey and I

are heading up north to check out a lead. I have my cell call me if you need us. Will do be safe. Did you find

out anything? Tommy asked Sarah. Yes, it seems that this town was used as a bit of a refuge town or a

hideout town through the years. The town below us was used the same apparently. Folk around here believe

it was a cover up or an assassination attempt gone wrong. Intriguing keep digging and let us know what you

find, be careful though were not sure whom we can trust yet. Will do Tommy, you and Harvey do the same.

Tommy meets Harvey and they head north. They arrive at Homers Drones manufacturing, a warehouse for

drones and remote-controlled toys. They pull in the drive a group of Spanish men were on break smoking.

As we walk to the door and open a young blonde at a desk asks; may I help you? I am Marshall Tommy Fuller and this my Deputy Harvey Coles. We need to speak to the owner or Manager. Hold please the lady named Carly hits the button and buzzes us in. We walk in the door and it shuts automatically behind us. Come in. A Russian male accent says. We walk to the desk and sit down as his face enters the light out of the dark room. He was a redheaded elderly Russian man. With an inviting smile on his face. What can I do for you? Gentlemen. We have this part and was wondering if it was familiar to you. Harvey places the remote shell onto the desk. Oh, yes, this is part of our remote four-wheel drive truck series, an extremely popular device used in the early 90's. Really? Tommy asked with some intrigue. Yes, here is one of the toys here. The owner Named Boris plops down a full-size replica of the semi that struck our town. May we take this? Yes, yes please if it helps you take it. We take the remote-controlled vehicle and walk back to the truck. We got our weapon we just have a needle in the haystack chance of finding the terrorist. Tommy cranks the vehicle and heads back. Harvey looks at his watch it was 5:30 he was a bit fidgety as an anxious boy about to go on his first date. This girl was not Harvey's girlfriend, but Samantha was special to him. He was falling for her. They arrive back at the station by 6:45 Harvey hops out and speaks to Sarah and Tommy. All the while watching his watch. Go on Harvey call her. See you in the morning yes sir. See you Sarah. See you Harvey give Samantha our regards. Harvey runs out the station hops in the car and dials the phone. Hello Samantha says with her sweet soft voice, Hi Harvey says. What are you doing? I was grading papers and listening to some hymns. What you up to? Just getting off work. Want to get a bite to eat with me? Sure, what time? I am in my truck now be there in about 30. Okay I will be ready. They hang up. Thirty minutes later he arrives at her door. A two-bedroom house with a white picket fence and yellow rosebushes surrounding the front of the house. He knocks on the door. Samantha a brunette who was an average size girl was dressed in a light blue dress that came about four inches below the knee, with a beautiful pearl necklace. With white tennis shoes on. Harvey had stopped by his house which was on the way and threw on some Jeans and a button up light blue shirt. On the way he stopped and got her a dozen red roses and a box of chocolate. As Samantha opens the door Harvey swallows and nearly faints at the beauty he sees. Samantha, sees the chocolate and flowers, and says for me? He says yes as he offers them to her. Thanks that is so sweet. But I really should not have candy I am a diabetic. Harvey turns white as sheet and apologizes. Samantha laughs. Gotcha! I am not a diabetic I was just kidding. Harvey smiles then he laughs. Good one he says. Where are we eating? Samantha asks. Dino's! What kind of place is that? It is an Italian restaurant. Awesome I love Italian food cannot wait let us go. Harvey escorts her to his truck and holds open the door and lets her in. They arrive at the restaurant and have a seat. They place an order, A lasagna for Harvey and Fettuccine and a salad for Samantha. Before eating they hold hands and Harvey asks the blessing. They begin eating and talking. They spend the evening together getting to know one another better. Once dinner is over, he takes her home and they sit in his truck and talk some more. Samantha you are such a beautiful smart caring woman. I really like you and would like it if you would be my girlfriend. I never have felt this way for anyone before, you are simply perfect for me. I do not want to ever let you go. I feel the same about you, I have liked you from the first day, you are such a handsome brave and gentle young man. And I love that fact you are a true believer in Christ. I would gladly be your girlfriend if there is a great possibility of more. Most definitely! I agree to be your girl then. Now shut up and kiss me. Samantha grabs him and they share a very intimate kiss. Harvey felt such a deep love and tenderness for her, Samantha felt great respect and passion for him. They fog up the windows and she pulled away and steps out. See you Sunday then? Yes, ma'am you sure will. I will come pick you up. Alright then drive safe officer. Good night Samantha Good night Harvey. Harvey drives home on cloud nine. He pulls into his driveway and notices something is off. He unholsters his gun and turns off the headlights. He

approaches his front door it had been busted open he eases into the house, papers and his stuff scattered. In

the back room of his house he hears someone rifling through his stuff. He eases towards the switchbox and

kills the power then he creeps towards the room and kicks in the door. Freeze! He hollers in the darkness, but

the window was opened, and the blind was torn down. Whoever it was must have gotten spooked and ran.

Harvey spends the next hour picking up the mess and finally around 3 falls asleep. The clock goes off at 7 and

he gets up and gets ready. When he arrives at the station, Tommy and Sarah are already there. They have a

concerned look and are busy searching databases and headlines. Good Morning Harvey says. Oh, morning

how was your date? Sarah asked. Date? Yeah, we saw you at Dino's last night with Samantha. How did you?

Harvey looked puzzled. We came in and saw you guys eating in the corner, we did not want to bother you, so

we just sat down and ate. So, how was it? It was good. We agreed to start dating officially. I say that was a

great date then. Sarah replied. Yeah, it was nice. Then why so gloomy this morning? Tommy asked.

Someone broke into my home when I got back, and they were still there when I went in. Did you see them

no they slipped out the back before I could catch them? Did they take anything? No, I do not think so I went

through and checked. I think they were looking for documents. Because they just ransacked my house and

did not even touch any of the high dollar items. But when they got into the old storage room in my house.

Where a lot of documents and papers from the previous owners are, they were searching for specific things.

This investigation keeps getting stranger and leading to more questions than answers. Did you fingerprint

home? No, I did not even think to do that! I did not touch the file room where they were, however. Good let

us get some prints and see who were dealing with. Alright then. Harvey rides back to his home to dust for

prints. To find that the perpetrators had retuned. This time Harvey locks the front door and blocks it with a chair on the outside. He radios Tommy and the heads around back. Sure, enough he sees them in there and was about to make his move when he feels a thump on the back of his head. Then all goes black! Later Tommy and Sarah get worried, they head to Harvey's to find the door open and a trail of blood out back. It led to some tracks and then dissipated. Someone had hit Harvey and had taken him hostage. We got to call for some help this is getting too deep. Tommy calls Captain Stevens and explains the situation. Stevens was able to find out some things that he shared with Tommy. We discovered that 20 years ago in your town Judge Matthews gave the maximum prison time to one Jethro Coles, a murderer, extortioner and mob boss. Who just happens to be the grandfather of your Harvey Coles? It seems Jethro upon doing his tours in Vietnam earned a bit of a reputation, as a king pin of sorts. You name it this guy was behind it. But he messed up one night. He rapes and kills Matthews Grand Daughter; He was then arrested by your father Tommy. So, you see this whole mess is based on one man's vendetta against your town and your father. He is still in jail and will be for the rest of his life. Due to the fact he was the one who leveled the town below you guys by unleashing a rocky avalanche burying a whole town. All because he got caught selling moonshine there. So, if he is in jail who is doing his dirty work. Harvey's dad mostly. But there are some of his mafia buddies involved. So, the whole truck bomb gas leak was all tied to us. Yes, afraid so. That family of three you found was in witness protection with new names s they just got careless and paid the price with their lives. Thanks Stevens can you put an APB out for Harvey's dad and help us bring him back. His girlfriend his head over heels for him. I do not want to have to tell her bad news, not to mention we do not want to lose him either. He is like a son to me and Sarah. I am glad you contacted me Tommy consider it done. We will inform you of any developments on our end. Thanks Jim, we appreciate the intel it fills in a lot of the blanks we had. I think we may know where to find them. Alright Tommy just call us if you need backup. 10/4 over and out. You think we will find them? Sarah asked. Yes, I do Harvey spoke of a cabin he and his dad would

fish at when he was a boy. It was located North of Denver. Let us keep this under wraps. No need to worry

Samantha just yet. I agree but he was going to pick her up for church Sunday. If he does not show she will be

worried, then. Your right just wait until 9am in the morning and we will both tell her. Just find the boy and

bring him home. Tommy pulls the address from Harveys personnel file and loads up and heads out. Sarah

stays behind to keep an eye on things. Tommy radios the address to Captain Stevens. Got it I will send two

squad cars to back you up. They will go in silent so as not to alert him. Tommy arrives at the property on the

back side near the lake he radios Stevens and instructs them to park a way and walk in from the sides and

the front. I will be in back. When you guys from the front get there. Knock on the door and then count to five

and come in. Patrols from the side make sure there are no surprises coming in. And cover all exits as well.

Harvey had spoken of an underground entrance to the cabin from the backyard. Tommy was hoping to find

and use this to gain access. The patrol men all reach the house it was just about sunset. Tommy finds the

entrance and sneaks in the house. He finds Harvey bound lying in a back bedroom near the underground

passage. He nudges Harvey tells him to remain quiet. He leads him down the hatch and out the back. Red

Dawg 2 the package is secure, I say again the package is secure. Upon saying that the police from the front

enter while the cops from both sides converge Bill, Harvey's dad was trapped. Along with ten other men in

the house. A gunfight ensues and fire breaks out and the cops scatter. Tommy and Harvey Guard the back as

the others hold there outside positions. One by one the men emerge hands in the air and knees on the

ground, the smoke was just too much. Harvey rides with Tommy while the police arrest his dad and his

thugs. He kidnapped me to spare me from the town. He said that they were going to level it just like they did

the one below. I do not know if I can take living in a town that could be leveled so easily anymore Tommy. I mean I am in love with Samantha and hope to marry her someday. I have passed the B.A.R and want to

practice defending the church in religious freedoms that the Christian face getting taken away. But the same

time you guys are like my parents. And I do not want to leave you guys here to face this alone. Harvey, son,

you must do what is best for you and your future family Sarah and I have duty to serve the folk in this

community and that is what we are going to do. You must choose your path and what you must do. God will

lead you if you allow him too. Besides, we will see you guys from time to time. Thanks, Tommy, Dad. They

arrive at Tommy and Sarah's and Harvey stays. He sets his alarm so as he would not miss out on picking up

Samantha. He lays down his head and the clock goes off before he knew it. He jumps up stretches and feels

like crap. But he was not going to let her down he jumps in shower its 8:45 am its 9 am when he gets out and

gets ready. Tommy was up and waiting to take him to his truck. They arrive at his house at 9:25 am it takes

him about twenty minutes to get to Samantha's he says goodbye to Tommy hops in his truck buys some

more flowers and a couple of sodas and heads over there. Samantha when she walked out was wearing a

pink solid dress with a matching flowery Jacket with matching shoes, she was so beautiful. Harvey wore his

Army suit with some black polished shoes. Harvey hopped out gave her the flowers and a kiss. She thanks

him for the roses, which were multicolored this time. And kisses him back. He compliments her on how

beautiful she is, she blushes and says thanks. You do not look half bad yourself. She says with a grin. Harvey

looks into her eyes and smiles. Sparks of true love twinkle in both their eyes. Better get going then. Oh,

yeah, he puts the truck in drive, and they head to church. It was good service, and the sermon was on

trusting in the Lord for all things. After the service some of Samantha's friends invited her and Harvey out to

eat. They spend the day together and part of the night just enjoying one another's company. I need to tell

you something Samantha. Harvey held her hand and looks into here deep blue eyes, Yes, what is it? I was mugged and kidnapped yesterday. What? You are kidding, right? Harvey's face said it all she knew he was

not. Why didn't you say something this morning and you could have rescheduled you must be exhausted?

Are you sure you are all right? Yes, I am. How did this happen? I mean I am sorry I do not mean to pry. I know

you guys cannot speak about job related things. No, it is okay Samantha this involved me personally and its

okay you deserve to know the story. Well it is like this: Harvey tells her all about his Grandfather and dad and

how all the stuff that had been going on was due to his family's vendetta. We caught the men and they went

to jail. Samantha sits in shock at all she just heard. Wow! She finally shouts. That is quite a story! It is all true

you can ask Tommy, Sarah, and Captain Stevens. No need for that I totally believe it. It is just so crazy you

know. Yeah, I know. Just found all this out myself. So, it is kind of new to me too, it is crazy. So, what now?

Are you going to stay on with Tommy or what? I have been praying and I believe it is time for me to start

practicing law as a lawyer. That is great to hear Harvey. I do not know what I would have done if something

had happened to you it scared me just to hear it. I knew it would, but I wanted you to hear from me not some

other source. That would have hurt you. Yeah, it would have. I appreciate your honesty and willingness to

share something like this with me. You are my soul mate why would I not. I love you Samantha. Oh, I love

you too Harvey. They hug and hold one another Harvey lays his head in Samantha's lap and falls asleep.

Samantha strokes his short brown hair and rubs his goat tee and says a prayer thanking God for bringing him

back to her safe. As she falls asleep. The clock strikes 7am and they both wake up. Good Morning Samantha

says in a cheery way. Good morning Samantha he says in a happy and playful way. I apologize for spending

the night over here, I just felt so peaceful I fell asleep. No worries, I did too. Want some breakfast before

work? Sure, why not. Samantha makes biscuits and gravy with sausage and eggs. They thank God for the

food then eat. Samantha must be work at 9 and Harvey at ten. So, they freshen up hug and kiss and agree to call one another at lunch. Harvey watches Samantha leave and gets in his truck. He grabs his phone five

missed calls. They were all from Tommy and Sarah. They just wanted to make sure he was okay, and they

would see him at work he arrives with donuts and smile. They thank him for the donuts with joy. How was

church? It was great we and some of her friends went out to eat. Afterwards we went to her place and

talked, I told her what happened. How did she respond? She was fearful for me, but glad I was okay. So, you

stayed over there? Yes, but not on purpose I fell asleep in her lap, Oh, you too are such a Roman tic couple.

Sarah says. Tommy says well, were glad you are okay. Now that this investigation is over, maybe we can all

relax some. By the way, what have you decided? I am pursuing my career in law as a defense lawyer for

church matters. That is great news Harvey! Sarah congratulates him and hugs him. I just want you guys to

know, it was not just because of what happened it has been a longtime desire of mine and I had been praying

for the right time. We never thought that Harvey. You do what God is leading you into. Just know were

behind your 100 percent. Both Tommy and Sarah agree.

Chapter 5

The dead tell the story

Harvey and Sarah and Tommy begin rebuilding the towns records and direct the carpenters on the restoring of the Courthouse. The hazmat came later that morning and began the cleanup operation. By lunch they had the parking lot clean of the chemical compounds. I am going to Lunch Sarah said. Tommy had left to inspect the barrier on the mountain. Alright Sarah, I will hold the fort down. Tell Samantha hi for me, will you? Harvey nodded and picked up the phone. He calls her and Samantha answers hello. Hey Samantha, Hi Harvey how is it going? Surprisingly good, got the tanker mess cleaned up and we have reorganized the courthouse documents. How about you? Its good some of the other teachers and I have gone to the local steak house for lunch. The kids were sent home early today for a renovation project on the school. Cool, have fun. Hey, want to hang out tonight? Sure, I can cook us dinner at my place. Sounds good Samantha. See you at 7 then? Yes, it is a date then. By the way Sarah said hi! Oh, tell her and Tommy I said hello. I feel as I have known them longer. Yeah, they have that effect on folks. Alright then, we will see you tonight. Alright Samantha I love you. I love you too Harvey, goodbye. They hang up and Sarah walks in. Did you have a good lunch? I did Sarah said. Have you seen or heard from Tommy? No, I thought he would have contacted you by now. Nope I was home for lunch and not a word. Let us call him. Sarah said grabbing her radio. Tommy come in, no answer. She tries again only to get static. He must be out of range lets head up to the mountain barrier and see if we can find him. Alright then, they hop in the truck and head up the mountain. They pull behind Tommy's SUV. They get out and walk up to the barrier. They reach the top and find Tommy. We tried to reach you. Sarah said. Oh, I am sorry the radio was on the fritz. Tommy was staring down at the ground. What have you found there, Tommy Harvey asked? Graves. Tommy replied. Graves? Harvey was puzzled. There are hundreds of shallow graves located just south of the barrier. Hundreds? Yes, there is an unmarked graveyard here. Did your father know anything of this? If he did, he was not talking

Harvey replied. What about yours? Nope, and I have lived here my whole life and never knew of or heard of

any graves. Let us check the records at the courthouse and see if we can find out who all maybe buried there.

Good idea we will head back now. You coming Tommy? Sarah asks. Yeah, I be there shortly I want to do

some more digging. Here is another radio then. Harvey hands him a new radio and Tommy turns it on and

tunes it to channel 4 that was the channel they were all on. Sarah kisses him and she and Harvey heads back.

They begin going through the files. It takes them to 5pm to go through them all. All three of them searched

through thousands of obituaries and had just about given up when Harvey found something. Here is a record

of an old coal mine near there that employed over 100 people. The mine caved in 100 years ago. The people

buried there worked in the mine. Interesting did they live here in town? No, they lived mostly in the lower

town. The one buried under rocks. That is the one, Harvey said. Well, how did these folk winds up here

buried if they lived down there? Guess they were killed in the collapse. Harvey said. The only way to be sure

is to exhume some of the bodies. Harvey looks at his watch its 6pm, got to go! Harvey says as he jumps up.

We will investigate this tomorrow then. Tommy says as they all head out the door. Alright we will get a team

up there in the morning and see what is going on in those graves. Alright Tommy see you at 8 am in the

morning then. Be safe and have fun with Samantha tonight. Will do she is cooking dinner tonight. I hear she

is an awesome cook Sarah said. She is or at least she can cook a mean breakfast so far this is all I can testify

to. Harvey gets in his truck and dials the phone. Hello Harvey. Hey Samantha, I am on my way running a little

behind need anything before I get there? Just you! Samantha says. Alright see you in a bit he hangs up. 30

minutes later at 7:30 Harvey pulls in. He gets out of the car and knocks on the door. Samantha answers

looking more beautiful than ever. He stares in awe of her beauty as she stares back him with excitement.

They stand there for a few minutes. Come in, come in. She invites him in and gives him a hug and a kiss.

Dinner is ready sir. She says in an English accent. Good I am starving! Harvey walks into the dining room to a candlelight table with pink roses and a white tablecloth. The table was already set. A homemade Lasagna and breadsticks and a salad lay waiting to be devoured, Harvey holds out the chair for her to sit and then sits himself and tucks a napkin in his shirt. Grabs her hand and bows his head. Lord, it thank you for Samantha who graciously prepared this food. I thank you for this food and this time together in Jesus' name I pray amen. Amen and dig in Harvey says they begin eating. This is delicious! Harvey exclaimed. If teaching does not pan out, you could open a restaurant. Samantha kicks him under the table and gives him a look like are you serious. Ouch, what was that for? Harvey rubs his leg. I thought you were being silly. And I worked hard for you and this meal. No, I am serious you are an excellent cook. Well thank you now finish your dinner, I have dessert. Dessert? Yes, its cheesecake! Samantha knew this was his favorite. Cheesecake! Harvey's eyes lit up! He finishes his meal and she brings out a big ole cheesecake with whipped topping, they share a piece and Harvey grabs the dishes. What are you doing? Samantha protested. I am cleaning up! You cooked I clean! Samantha after much disputation agreed to let him. She blew out the candle and played some hymnal music in the background. How was your day? Harvey asked as he loads the dishwasher and puts up the leftovers. It was good. You know they let the kids go home early for a renovation project. Yeah, I remember you telling me this at lunch. Well when we got back, we were asked to take the rest of the day too as they were painting the classrooms. So, I went shopping and got all this together. It was wonderful too thanks so much. Your welcome. Samantha said. They sit together on her nice microfiber couch. She asks him about his day, and he tells her of the graves. How bizarre she says. They look at each other and begin to kiss. They stop themselves in the heat of the moment and Samantha hops up and fixes herself and asks. Want to watch a movie? Sure thing. Harvey says. She opens Amazon prime and they pick a movie. When the movie is over

Harvey gets up, I really must go. I must be at work at 8 am and I have not seen the inside of my home since the abduction. Do not go Samantha pleads, I would feel better if you did not go home. I need to get some clothes and such I need a shower and I need to check my mail. I know it is just I worry so since you were kidnapped and all, it will be fine. Harvey tries to reassure her, but she persisted. He agreed to stay the night and go by his house tomorrow evening with her. She just did not want to let him out of her sight. They sit back on the couch and hold each other late into night. Harvey ponders the events of the day. And knows he cannot let this girl go, and they cannot keep doing this it just was not right, and it could lead to more wrongs. Even though he loved her, and she loved him. To make love prior to marriage would be against God. And he could not do this. He knew he wanted to marry her. So, he spent the next hour planning on how to purpose. He fell asleep. The next morning, he woke before she did it was Saturday morning. He left her a note and went to work. Before heading in though he stopped by his house and took a shower and changed into his clean uniform and put on a load of laundry. He arrives at the station. The gravediggers had already arrived and so Had Tommy. They were on site carefully digging up the graves. By 10 am they were all dug up. They began digging through the bodies and looking for clues. Upon examination of several of the bodies it was apparent they did not die in the cave in. They were all executed by a single gunshot in the head. Upon further investigation the discovered they were all Asian. Apparently, the mining company had hired some Chinese workers and wanted to cover up the whole mining accident. Upon inspection of their outfits they detected chemical. It was apparent these men and women were not killed and buried 100 years ago as they had assumed. They were killed and buried only a few years ago. About the same time the stones destroyed the lower village. Upon further investigation it was apparent These men and women were all geologists sent to investigate the disturbances in the mountain. Interesting, so they must have discovered something that got them killed. But what would that be? After digging we found that the cave had been dug out and a chemical dumpsite had been made. The rocks were placed to cover this up, they knew no one would investigate a pile of rubble. So, they killed the geologists and buried the town along with their secrets. They would have gotten away with it to had Tommy not uncovered the graves. Truly the dead told the story. The company unnamed for identity purposes, was fined and the men in charge from the killers to the CEO were arrested and the once buried secret had been revealed the hazmat team came and cleaned up the mess. Harvey checked his phone, one missed call, one voice mail. It was Samantha. He dials the voicemail. Hi honey, I mean Harvey. I got your message hope to see you this evening call me. After filling out the paperwork it was 4:30pm. Go ahead and go Harvey I know you want to talk to Sam. Sarah; Tommy I would like to discuss something with you guys. Go ahead. Tommy and Sarah look to him with anticipation. It is about Samantha; I have fallen in love with her and cannot stand to be away from her. I have spent the past two nights over there and I want to spend every night with her. So, your saying you want to marry her? Yes, but it has just been three weeks since we met, and I just wanted your thoughts on the matter. Well, I do not believe there has to be a certain amount of time to date before you marry. It was not done that way in the Bible and it is just society that says date awhile, or do not even marry. Obviously, you two love one another very much and are equally yoked. I think you should propose, and I have the perfect ring it was your mothers ring. It is a ¼ Carat diamond engagement ring princess cut. The diamond is 80% clarity and would retail for 3,000 or more. I would be honored to give this to her. Since Tommy and I cannot have children you have been our son. Even though were only 23 years older you are still our son. For sure you have been my parents and it means a lot. Thanks so much. I am going to need a week off I want to take a trip with her to Hawaii. I have been saving for this vacation and now that I have someone to take it with, its time. Take all the time you need. Tommy said. So, when you going to leave us for the Courtrooms? I start my internship in the fall and hope to stay on until I land my own practice. Sounds like you have it all figured out. Better call Sam. It was 5:30 and he calls her. Hey baby, I mean Samantha. Is it okay if I call you Sam or baby? Sure, if I can call you honey, Harvey. So, what is up? You got time off coming right? The school has shut down for the summer for a complete overall. Perfect! Pack your backs for a week. A week? Where are we going? Hawaii! What? She screamed with excitement nearly busting his eardrum. Are you for real? Yes, I have been saving for three years for this trip I have already made the flight reservations and have booked us a nice motel on the beach of Honolulu. I will be there in a half an hour to pick you up. Okay honey, I cannot wait I am so excited. Alright baby I will see you in a bit. Harvey pulls into his driveway and grabs his back from the garage and packs some clothes and other necessary items. It puts the ring box in his carpenter jean pocket and seals it up. Harvey showers and shaves with great anticipation. Two hours later they are at the airport in Denver. Flight 3471 Honolulu departing at 9pm in South gate 23. The announcer says on the intercom. The Gate they needed was on the other side of where they were, they had to hurry. They got there just in time and gave their tickets to the stewardess. We are going! Samantha teared up with joy. She had long since dreamed of this moment but thought it would never happen. But it was happening now and with the man she loved dearly. She thought within herself is he doing all this to purpose. Know I want him too and my friends were excited for me. That I had found love. I know he does not want to continue spending the night at my place not being married. She pondered these thoughts as she held tight to his arm and leaned her head on his shoulder. He let her have window seat, but she was content with the view she had beside her. She only hoped they would return either engaged or married. She hoped for the latter as she could not bear spending a night away from him, she wanted to be with him always. She fell asleep with her head on his shoulder.

Harvey thought of ways to propose and had hoped to find a wedding chapel and be married upon returning. But he was not sure how she felt if she would want to wait. All he knew is he could not keep sleeping over there with her not being married. He knew the sin it would lead to and he loved her too much for this. As a man he wanted her bad but had to abstain but could no longer be with her without being married. So, this trip was important.

Chapter 6

The arrival

The plane lands and Harvey nudges Samantha and says. Were here! Yay! Sam throws up her hands and shouts. She could not wait to get off the plane. Folk looked at her funny for shouting. This is her first trip here and mine too. Were just excited. The passengers nodded and went about their exiting the plane. Finally, Sam and Harvey step out of the plane on the island of Hawaii they rent a car and drive up the road to the beach hotel. The hotel was a five-star hotel complete with valet parking and the works they settle in their two-bed motel room, and head out. Harvey saw on the way to the motel a beautiful location with a waterfall nearby. He drives to the location and they exit the car and sit on a rock viewing the waterfall. It truly was a sight to see. Sam, this past three weeks have been

the best three weeks of my life since knowing you. I never knew I could find a love like this. You have

stolen my heart and have knitted my soul to yours. When I am away from you, I feel incomplete. The

past couple of times we spent the night in each other's arms showed me how much I love and want

to be with you the rest of my days. When I kiss your lips, it takes my breath away. When you touch

me, my senses come alive like never I have felt. I love you and want to: he bows on one knee and

pulls out the ring. And asks her to marry him. Samantha is bawling with joy and grabs him saying

yes, yes, yes. She kisses him and he puts the ring on her finger. This was my mother's engagement

ring I want you to have it if you accept it. If? Of course, it is beautiful! I would be honored to wear it.

Now that is over, I have another surprise! What? She giggles with excitement as she sees a band of

Hawaiian band members come with flour laulaus and place them on their necks. A big shouldered

man comes up to us and asks who wants to be married. Harvey says we do! Samantha is amazed

and awestruck her wildest dreams were coming true. And her soulmate was making them happen

through his faith in God. She was elated she could not stop weeping with joy this would be a day to

remember for the rest of her life. The minister begins to ceremony explaining that the wedding ring

was a symbol of the eternal love God has for us. And how our love should be an everlasting love for

each other. The wedding was magnificent! Later there was a feast and yes there was a whole pig on

the rotisserie. The wedding celebration continued into the evening until the left and went for a walk

on the beach. The waves crashed on the beach as they walked along. I cannot believe this!

Samantha screamed. Believe what? Harvey asked. Here we are in Hawaii hand in hand as a married

couple. I never dreamed this would happen this way in a million years. We get married and get to spent four days on honeymoon in paradise! This is what people write romance novels about. Yet here we are an officer of the law and Lawyer intern and schoolteacher walking the beaches of the most beautiful place on earth. They spend the evening on the beach in silence just holding one another. Then go back to room. They were married now they began making out and wound up in bed. The next morning, they woke and looked at each other. Good morning Honey Samantha says as she caresses his beard. Good morning baby he replies. Yesterday was special and will ever be in my memories. Mine too baby, mine too. They crawl out of bed and go to the bathroom and get ready. The spend the next four days sailing, deep sea fishing and scuba diving. They dine at some of the most exquisite restaurants and their love grows stronger each day. Friday comes and it is time for them to depart they had the wedding party take pictures with their cameras. They also took lots of pictures on the honeymoon. Memories that would stay with them forever. Back at the airport they arrive check in hurry up and wait. Samantha texts her friends with a picture of the wedding and the ring. With the words, We Did IT! Harvey dials Tommy and lets him know how it went. Congratulations Harvey and Samantha. Harvey heard Sarah squealing with excitement. Sarah calls her mom who lived in Georgia. Harvey heard squealing and laughter and congratulations. Everyone was happy they were married.

Chapter 7

The departure

They board the plane as husband and wife, they came as boyfriend and girlfriend. Now they would return to spend their life as a family. The question was where to live. They discuss this on the plane. I think we should live in your house. Harvey said. Are you sure she asked? Yes, it is closer to the city where my internship will be. Plus, all your stuff is already there. I have less stuff to move than you, so it makes sense. We will use your furniture because everything you have is nice. I will just set up my office in the basement bonus room. Her house had a finished basement. It was the best choice for them, so they agree. They would go home rest go to church Sunday and then Sunday afternoon move his clothes and office to her home. Upon arriving in Denver, they find their bags and are taken to their car via transit when they reach his truck the load their bags and souvenirs for their friends and family. They head home and arrive as they approach the house Harvey snatches her up and unlocks the door and carries her over the threshold. A couple of hours later he unloads the car. Ad they spend the night together in each other's arms. The next day was Sunday they get up and head to church. They are greeted with a mob of church members and surprise housewarming party after the service. The pastor introduced them as a new family, and it was a grand ole day. They spend the day with friends and the pastor and his wife. They get to know Harvey and his plans. They were intrigued by his desire to serve the church in this way. They spent the afternoon socializing and getting to know each other. After the day was over, they head home and swing by his house he grabs what he needs and puts a for sale sign on his property.

They go home and chill on the couch watching TV then go to bed. The next morning Harvey wakes to Samantha cooking breakfast. He gets up and gets dressed He sees Samantha cooking in his T-shirt and some shorts. He hugs her from behind and says good morning, Baby. Morning Honey, breakfast will be ready in a few. Your holster gun, and keys are hanging by the door and I packed you a lunch. Oh, thanks baby. Your welcome Honey now come eat. Harvey sits sips some coffee and looks at the local paper. Local Pastor arrested for refusing to submit his sermons. This, here is why I want to desperately defend the rights of the church. I know honey, just take one day at time and the Lord will give you the desires of your heart if you keep him first. I know It just burns me up when I reads or hear something like this. You will have your chance just wait for the Lord and you will succeed. Words of wisdom baby, words of wisdom. Thanks, I needed that. Your welcome. Now give me some sugar. Harvey reaches over and kisses her. Need help cleaning? No, you need to get to work you are going to be late! Oh, shoot! Harvey looks at his watch. He has 35 minutes to get ready and leave and drive to get there right on time. Harvey throws on his holster checks his gun and kisses Sam goodbye and heads out the door and phones Tommy. Good morning Harvey. Morning I am on my way may be a tad bit late. Thanks for calling see you soon.

Chapter 8

A horrible discovery

Upon arriving at the station, he is greeted with a banner that says congrats! Once inside

Sarah hugs him and Tommy hugs him too. They hand him an envelope and invite Sam and

he to dinner tonight. I will need to ask her buy I thinks she would be game. By the way have

you heard from Linda? Linda had been seen with her sister on the big restoration day that

led to the truck wreck. Harvey noticed she had not been seen or heard from since. Thanks

for reminding us, shamefully, with all the excitement around here I plum forgot about her.

Sarah said as she picked up the phone. She called Julie her sister's number no answer she

called Linda's number and got a busy signal as if the phone were off or unplugged. She

called the neighbor next door to Julie and asked them had they seen them out. No, we have

not but heard a motor running all night the other night then it finally quit. Thanks. Sarah

hangs up. I think we should go out there. Harvey and I will go you stay and hold down the

fort. We are not sure what we may see. Harvey and Tommy head to the SUV and head over

to Julie's. Upon arriving the smell gas all inside the house, they put on masks and open all

the doors when they walk to the car the find Linda and Julie both dead in their cars, they

had turned black and had begun decomposing. Apparently, both were severely depressed.

Upon further investigation of the home, they find three small children Julie's kids had been murdered it appeared Pryor to apparent suicide. But after seeing the signs of struggle and noticing the bodies of Linda and Julie they discovered this was no suicide. It was household homicide. We call the coroner's office and have them come remove the bodies for further autopsy. We dust the home for prints and examine the windows for any forced entry or exit. It was apparent they knew the suspect. Hopefully, the prints would tell us who. They fax the prints to the crime lab in Denver. They head back to Sarah and deliver the news. No! Who, who would want to kill those sweet ladies and their kids? What monster would do such a thing? That is what we hope to find out. Later that they Harvey gets the results via e-mail. The prints belong to three men. One Javier Lopez, Enrique Hernandez, And Carlos Santorini. Wait those names ring a bell! Tommy pulls up the most wanted list. There their names were. They were part of a rogue Mexican cartel that dealt in human trafficking for slave labor and for prostitution. A bad group of folks to mess with. But what did Julie and Linda and her children have to do with these guys? I think I know Sarah commented. Let us hear it then. Tommy inquired. Well, Julies husband worked with a task force that rescues these girls from these slimeballs and gives them a new life. Guess he got too close to the fire, and they nailed his family. Poor Linda was just killed because of being there. This is too much to handle on our own. If these folks can come and do this here, they have a lot of connections. The FBI needs to handle this one. They all agree and make the call. The agent in charge had been tracking these guys and appreciated the tip and sent their condolences. Sarah was pretty torn up by this she could not believe this had happened. It was terrible to think of such a small mountain town as this. Later the FBI agent came by she was a tall slender fair looking lady. She walked into the station she introduced herself. Hello, I am Special agent Nicole Simpson and you must be? Marshall Tommy and this is deputy Marshall Harvey at your service. I need to see the report on what you guys found and any autopsy reports. Sure, thing here you go. Harry hands her the reports. She looks them over intently for several minutes. What do you think? Tommy asked to finally break the silence. It is our guy that we have been tracking. These two were had traces of heroin in their blood. Which tells me your Linda and Julie were once in his brothel. He would pump them full of heroin and keep them high so they would not escape. These girls did, Harvey chimed in. Yes, they did Nicole replied. But how? Linda's husband ran a rescue mission which rescued sex trafficked people from their captors. Tommy informed her. I see, this all makes sense! What does? Harvey asked. All the things that have happened here that is. The gas leak, the family burned to a crisp, the truck incident and your kidnapping. O, that was my grandfather and my dad. Harvey replies. That is what they wanted you to think. Nicole says. Tommy and Harvey stand mouths open and dumfounded. This was all orchestrated by Carlos the viper as he is called. He and Julio and Enrique have been on a tear lately. They paid the chemical company to assassinate the geologists because they discovered their drug operation in the cave not a chemical dumped by a company but heroin production. When they discovered they knew they had them killed and the rockslide bury the lower town. They have kidnapped girls and boys and sold them into slavery and have been responsible for over a thousand drug related deaths in the United States alone because of their drug and sex trafficking operations. When they found out you had arrested their cover operation men. They did some digging and found out that you, Harvey was connected to your grandfather and dad's crimes. They used your dad to implement their dirty work to derail you guys from their trail. Also because of your dad they discovered Mrs. Linda and Julie's location. So, does that explain what things? Nicole asked Harvey and Tommy. Yes, it does. Wow you guys have been paying attention then. Yes, and now we know they are in the area it gives us a good lead. Let no one know outside of the three of you who and what I am. And Harvey you should move your wife in with Sarah and Tommy A.S.A.P! she could be in danger as well Samantha! He grabs his phone and call her. Hey honey what is up? Hey baby I am going come get you and I need you to pack a few things were going to be staying in town with Tommy and Sarah. Why? I will explain later just be ready. Okay I love you; I love you too Harvey. He hangs up runs to his truck and flies to their home he gets there in record time. As he pulls into the drive, he sees a black SUV slowly driving by and Samantha is coming out the door. Get Down! Harvey screams and runs to her and throws her down gets on top of her just as he does the window on the SUV rolls down and the barrel of an AR-15 comes out and bullets start flying. They strike the door of the house and Harvey's truck. As the car speeds away, Harvey jumps up firing at the truck and gets the license plate number off the tag as they sped away, he calls the city police department and gives them the number and then calls Tommy. He goes over to Samantha who had already gotten up. She was shaking and tears were falling down her face. What, why? She could barely breathe let alone speak. Are you hurt? Tommy asked. She shook her head no. Tommy hugs her and wipes her tears. Let us go quickly they get in the bullet riddled truck and head back up the mountain to station on the way back Harvey tells her everything as she sits in silence. Samantha breaks down sobbing, poor Linda, Julie. You all are going to catch these guys, right? Well it is in the FBI's hands and the state police. But we will keep up with the case while we keep you safe. They must be stopped Samantha snapped. Yes, they do and all of us together will stop them. I sure hope you do. These men are so evil and those poor girls. They arrive at Tommy and Sarah's. Samantha walks in and Sarah runs and hugs her. I am so glad your safe. Sarah says as she hugs her neck. Harvey walks over to the station where Tommy and agent Nicole were. Glad you're okay Harvey. Samantha? Tommy asks. Harvey nods to let him know she was. Did you write the number down to SUV? Nicole asked. Yes, I did here. He hands her the number. She notifies her office and has them run the tag number. I gave the number to Captain Stevens as well. Good the more we have looking the better chances we have of finding them. A few minutes later her office calls. Oh, okay thank you, she says as she wrote something down. When she hung up, she approaches Tommy and Harvey. The SUV was registered to one Douglas Benito. He lives just outside Denver he owns a used car lot called Benito's. Let us go check it out then. Tommy says. No sir we need you two to stay put in case they come through here. I have backup meeting me there.

Tommy and Harvey reluctantly agree

Chapter 9

The Chase

Harvey and Tommy head back to his house. Sarah and Samantha are watching videos and laughing. They come in and are greeted by a hug. Sarah hugs Tommy and Samantha kisses and hugs Harvey. What you guys watching? Some home videos of you no doubt. What? Yeah, there your high school and police academy videos. Very funny! Harvey smiles and blushes. We made pizza for you guys hope you're hungry. Hungry? Were famished. Tommy rubs his tummy and licks his lips. Sarah brings the homemade meat lover's pizzas to the table. Harvey and Tommy remove their hats. You do the honors. Tommy motions to Harvey. Lord, we thank you for keeping Samantha and I safe and for being with Sarah, Tommy and I as we spoke to the FBI. I pray that you would prosper them on their investigation and help them bring these evil men to justice. For we know that you know where they are, and your vengeance will be swift on them. We pray for their souls that they would repent and be saved. Not our will Lord but thine be done. Thank you, Lord, for this food and for Samantha and Sarah who prepared it. Now make it good for us to eat in Jesus' name I pray amen. Amen dig in I say. Tommy says as he grabs a slice and sips his Dr. Pepper. Unbelievably delicious ladies Tommy says with his mouth half full. Harvey grabs a slice and takes a bite, Yes, I agree it yummy indeed. Thirty minutes later they finish. I will clean up Harvey says as he grabs their plates and cups. He begins washing the dishes and wiping down the table. Tommy sits on the couch by Sarah. Looks like you have him trained already. Sarah smiles. No, he just does that own his on Samantha replied. He has the you cook I clean or vice a versa thing. Yeah, he has always been helpful even as a young boy. We raised from the time he was 6 on up. You have a good man in Harvey. I know I do Sarah; I know I do. Samantha replies as Harvey sits down. And I have the most wonderful wife in the world. Harvey

says flatteringly. Harvey and Sam sit together on the love seat while Tommy and Sarah are on the couch.

They talk, laugh and have a good time for hours. The phone rings at 9pm. Tommy answers. Hello. Yes, this

agent Nicole giving you an update. We arrived at the dealership and it was a dead end there was sign of the

SUV are any other car. The office had been cleaned out and there was not even a scrap of paper on the floor.

We dusted for prints and saw some tire tracks and footprints were following them to see where it leads.

Keep your family close and be alert they could come after you all. I have sent some extra agents to watch

over you and your family. They will arrive in the morning. Until then you guys are on your own. Stay safe.

You too and catch those guys, will you? We will do or best Marshall, I know you guys will. Tommy replies as

he hangs up. Who was that Tommy? It was Nicole the FBI agent they hit a dead end at the dealership but

found some tire tracks that might lead them to where they went. An hour later Harvey's phone rang. This is

Deputy Harvey. Yes, this Captain Stevens. We found your black SUV. Where? Boulder Colorado outside of

town at an abandoned warehouse. Our guys have brought it in if you guys want to check it out in the

morning. I will let you know Captain. Call me Jim, Harvey. Okay Jim thanks for the tip. Harvey hangs up.

What did he say? Sarah and Tommy and Sam looked at him. He said they found the black SUV. Where?

Outside of Boulder in an abandoned warehouse about hour from here, He wanted to know if we wanted to

see it in the morning. You bet we do all three of them said. Harvey looked at Sam with a puzzled face. You

do not think I am going to sit here while you go look at it do you? No mam I do not. That settles it then, we

all go in the morning. It will be the best way to watch out for each other and help us keep from going insane

over this. Alright then it is getting late this old man is going to bed. Not without your old lady Sarah stands

and yawns. Well come on old lad let us give the young'uns some quiet time. Sarah tells them good night and says I am coming old man. Harvey and Sam sit and hold one another in silence her head on his shoulder his head on hers. The silence lasts for a few minutes. How are you holding up babe? Harvey asks. Not too good but I will be alright if you are with me.

Always baby, always. Harvey says softly as he kisses her forehead. Let us go to bed. Sam whispers. Harvey agrees it was now midnight. They walk hand in hand into the spare room Harvey's old room. And they snuggle tight and fall fast asleep. In the morning Harvey is awakened to the smell of sausage and eggs and biscuits cooking. Harvey gently removes his arm from her waist and creeps out of bed. She grunts and says. What's that smell? Breakfast! She squeals as she hops out of bed beating him to the kitchen, Need any help? She asked. Nope, its already done just have a seat and we will eat. Tommy stumbles in from down the hall from their bedroom. You kids sleep okay? Yes, sir we did. Sam replies. No need to call me sir Just Tommy will do. Okay tommy will do. Sam said jokingly. Tommy, Sarah, and Harvey laugh. You're quite the comedian aren't you. Nah, just used to being around fourth graders. I still think your funny Sarah says. Me too Harvey replies. Yes, you sure are. Tommy confirms. They say grace over the food and Harvey and Samantha cleanup. While they clean Tommy calls Captain Stevens and informs him, they were coming. Alright Tommy see you soon Jim replied as he hung up. Jim talks to his officers and informs them that Marshalls Tommy and Sarah and Deputy Harvey and his wife Samantha are coming to inspect the vehicle. So, let them all in when they arrive. Yes, sir we will. Meanwhile Tommy and crew all load up in his Chevy Suburban. An hour later they arrive. Hello, were here to see the SUV. And you are the lady receptionist asked. We are the Marshalls who spoke with Captain Stevens. Oh, just let them in Carla. Jim sasses her. Yes sir. She snips back as he motions them back. Sorry about Mr. Black she can be handful. I bet. Sarah added. I trust your trip from Fort Collins was nice. Yes, it was quite pleasant. Tommy replied. Let's see it then. He leads them to the police impound garage and there it sat. Samantha gripped

Harvey's hand hard. As she swallowed hard. The memory of the drive by shooting came flooding back.

Harvey patted her on the back to reassure her, that it was okay he was there. Did you find anything? Tommy

asked. We did. We found shell casings and bullets holes from Harvey's gun in the back of the vehicle. We also

found large amounts of blood. It seems one of them took a bullet from Harvey's gun. The gunman were just

flunkies sent by Carlos. They were unknown to our files both local and federal. In fact, no record of them at

all. Your saying they were wiped from records? Yes, some black ops unit. This keeps getting stranger by the

day. What would a black ops unit be doing working for Carlos. Probably mercenaries. These military types

hire themselves out to the highest bidder. They offer their services as military advisers; hit men and

kidnappings and any other thing they can make a buck. It will be hard tracking these guys down. They are

good about covering their tracks. We keep on it though something is bound to turn up. Harvey thought back

to his time spent in the military. His sister Nicole had mentioned a black ops unit called the Wolverines. That

were operating in the Midwest. Harvey thinking of how he missed Nicole his sister. He found it odd that the

Agent's name was Nicole also. And she also was the same build! Harvey pondered this could it be? Later

that evening Nicole phones in. The tracks led to an old farmhouse. We are sending agents there in the

morning. We found the SUV! Tommy chimed in. You did? Well the Denver police did. But we saw it. It seems

some black ops unit was involved. Tommy added. Black ops? The Wolverines! Nicole shouted. I knew it!

They have been working in the Midwest for some time now. How's Harvey and Sam holding up? She asks.

Their doing okay. And Sarah? She's doing well she is quite the rock when things get hard. That's good.

Nicole replied. You seem really invested in our wellbeing. More than most agents would be. Why is this? I

cans tell you now. But just tell Harvey go Wolverines! For me if you will. Sure! Tommy said. Keep us in the loop. Will do Nicole said. Tommy scratched his head. Go Wolverines? What could this mean? And what was her interest in Harvey and Sam? He had to know. Harvey, Yes Tommy? I spoke with Nicole just now. She said they the trail led to a farmhouse. And she had agents checking it out in the morning. She also said to tell you Go Wolverines! She did? I knew it! Knew what? Both Tommy and Sam and Sarah asked. Samantha thought she may have been an old girlfriend of Tommy's, so you asked. No, baby I haven't dated anyone but you since high school. Well who is she to you? Tommy was dying to know. She sure seems to care a lot for this family. That is because she is family! Harvey stated. How so? Tommy asked and Sarah and Sam were curious. She is my SISTER! Sister? Sarah screamed. Yes, Nicole Faith Coles! Are you sure? Samantha asked. Yes, she and I watched the movie Red Dawn about these young kids helped fight off a Russian invasion and they would yell Wolverines! It was the name of their high school football team. Anytime we would speak to each we would holler this phrase at the end of our conversation. Wow that's Awesome honey. Maybe you get to speak to her more. Yeah, this is cool. Harvey says. They sit down to dinner, meatloaf and a salad. That Sam and Sarah fixed together. After dinner they ate dessert a homemade cheesecake that Samantha made. They play few rounds of Uno and hit the sack. Samantha and Harvey hold one another tight. Sam whispers love me tonight and they turn out the light. The next morning Harvey awakes and puts on his clothes Sam grabs the sheet and runs to the bathroom in their bedroom he had one in his room. She came out dressed to kill a few minutes later Harvey whistles. You look so beautiful. Thanks Honey You look purdy too. She says and grins. Thanks babe. Tommy had stepped out on the porch to grab some wood for the fire as it had snowed and was quite cold. He comes in with no wood and a worried look on his face. What is it? Sarah asked. Tommy was white as sheet he was in shock! Sarah scrams for Harvey! Harvey and Sam come running out. Sarah had Tommy on the couch. What is wrong? Harvey asked. He went outside to get some wood for the fire. When he came, he was in shock? Harvey grabs his gun and runs out the door. Laying in the snow

was a dead dear. Its head was on the front steps with a note attached to the antlers. We know where you

live, and we can get to you when want to. So, back off are you will regret it. If you live to that is! Harvey dials

Nicole and tells her the news. She sounded worried. Are you guys okay? Yes, but this is scary I must admit.

Harvey replies. I know bro, I mean Harvey. It's okay sis I know who you are. Whew, I knew you would figure It

out. You always were quite the detective. So, were you! Harvey responds. What do you guys want to do? I

think we should go somewhere safe. I don't want nothing happening to Sam. Nor do I or you or Tommy or

Sarah. Do they know? Yes, I told them when he said Go Wolverines! That was cool! Harvey says. I knew you

didn't recognize me at first. No, it didn't register at first. I recognized you right away. You haven't changed

much. No, I haven't but you have. Yeah, the service has a way of doing that. How did you become an FBI

agent? Well, it was about a 6 months ago when I was in Kuwait. I was contacted by an FBI recruiter regarding

the Wolverines. I had done some operations over there with the group. I knew a lot about them so they

asked me would I want to work on the case and others and an FBI agent. I agreed and here I am. I live in

Denver and our field office is there also. I have a home there that is in a gated community with 24-hour

security by the police. Plus, I have a live feed of my property going directly to our office. Where we have

people monitoring it around the clock. Plus, I have two Pitbull guard dogs in my backyard with a 10ft high

electric fence around it. Not the mention I have two boxers that live inside with me. Daisy and Rocky. It

sounds like a fortress. Harvey says. It is. I had to set up security due to some threats against our office awhile

back. I could bring you guys into protective custody. If it would be agreeable to the misses. We wouldn't

want to impose. It's no trouble Harvey. Besides, it will give me a chance to get to know Sam. And Tommy

and Sarah. You know Tommy isn't going want to just lie down and hide. Harvey states. Oh, I know I have kept a watch on you over past few years. When mom died and dad dropped you off at my home. I knew Sarah from a way back. I knew she would raise you as her own and so would Tommy. But I constantly kept tabs on you. You're my baby brother and I love you so much. Talk to Tommy, tell him he can help us remotely from my home by gathering more info on the whereabouts of the Wolverine they call Big John. He is the one that could lead us to Carlos and his men. I will tell him and thanks Nicole. I will call you at lunch to let you know when I am coming to pick you up. You're picking us up? Yes, it's too risky to send anyone else. Carlos has men within the departments. Good point. Harvey said. Plus, I want to get a chance to meet my brother's wife. Of course. Harvey replied. She is a beautiful lady how did you get so lucky. Nicole asked. It wasn't luck it was just meant to be. God sent her to me. I know he did it's the only way you could have found such woman as her. Gee thanks. Harvey replies. I meant that where you live and work there wasn't much opportunity for finding love like hers in the field you work. True it wasn't easy finding anyone to date. But then again, I wasn't looking. Alright Harv. I got to let you go. I have a lot of planning to do and so do you. Alright Nicole see you soon. You bet! Bye. Nicole and Harvey hang up. After all this it was now 10 am. So, Harvey had to gather them around and give them the news. Tommy finally had calmed down enough to speak. After Harvey told them of Nicole's offer, they agreed. Tommy was reluctant at first but then when Harvey explained he could search for Big John. He went along. Samantha was excited to meet Nicole. After Harvey let her know she wanted to meet her. Sarah was stoked to meet her friend. Sarah, Tommy, Harvey, and Sam began packing their clothes and necessary things. At 12:01pm Nicole calls. You all ready? Yes, we are. Good I will be there shortly. Within an hour she arrived in a blacked-out Lincoln Navigator accompanied by three other SUV's. She gets out comes to the door. Ready? She asked. We are Tommy said. They all load into Nicole's Lincoln and head out. On the way from Fort Collins they head to Nicole's home in Denver. On the way. It's so good to see you my friend. Sarah said. It's good to see you too Sarah. And Sam, may call you

Sam? Yes, you may. It nice to meet you. Nicole says. It's nice to meet you too. Tommy says it's good to see

you again also. For sure Tommy. Nicole says. Also, they went to House we found and there was a shootout

and some of our agents were killed and others injured. We had to send back up and were finally able to

prevail over the enemies. When we able to penetrate the House, we found about ten women in the

basement in a cell that we were able to free. It seems that they were some of the Wolverines who were killed

in the standoff. We knew this by the insignias on their coats, a wolverine. We also found heroin, weapons

and contact numbers to one of the three commanders Enrique. This is a break in the case. But we have a

long way to go. So, Tommy I have you an office with an outside line to Captain Stevens us and any other

entity you need. We will keep you in the loop via video conferencing with you and Harvey and Sarah.

Together we will stop these men. They pull into her neighborhood the escort vehicles back off and set up a

perimeter. They pull into her garage and exit the vehicle. Let me go prep My babies and get them pinned up

so you get overwhelmed at first. Tommy had questionable look on his face. Babies? My boxers! Nicole

replies. Oh, okay Tommy said. She goes in and they hear her sweet talking the dogs. A few minutes later she

opens the door. Come on in. Nicole holds the door as the enter the house. Nice place you have here Sarah

and Sam both compliments. The home was a two story with a finished basement the windows on decorative

bars on the outside. There was a large living room and a smaller TV Room, a large dining room with a long

oak table in the middle. A crystal chandelier hung over the table. The kitchen had a mobile landing in the

middle, the appliances were stainless steel the fridge was a smart fridge and the faucets were voice

activated. Her colors in the kitchen were teal and white. She had a picture of her a Harvey over the fireplace

in the living room. The whole house was hooked into Alexa. The television, the lights and the locks on the door as well as the doorbell camera. The TV was a 75-inch 4k HDTV with surround sound speakers surrounding the room. Upstairs and downstairs there were four bedrooms all together. In the basement was an office complete with a 70-inch monitor on the wall with state-of-the-art equipment and computers. The office was sealed as a bunker and an underground exit tunnel into the woods behind her home. She had thought of everything. And was prepared. It was the safest home they could stay in. Make yourself at home. Help yourself to anything you need I took the liberty of buying two months' worth of food and supplies. Just in case it took longer than expected to catch them. They settle in it was now 3 pm they began getting used to the basement office equipment while Nicole heads to the office in Denver. Around 4pm she video calls in. Tommy, Harvey, Sarah. She greets them. Where is Sam? She asked. She is upstairs playing with the dogs. She loves dogs. That's good. Nicole says. Well, just checking in. I'm sending you what we have on Big John. Okay, I got thanks. If you need me, just hit the camera on your monitor and it will call me directly. Catch you guys later. By the way do you guys like Chinese food? Yes, we do. Good I get off at 7 tonight I will bring us some home. It was 5pm. Tommy looks over the data they had on Big John and his last known whereabouts. Turns out he owned a junkyard in Boulder, and he hung around a motorcycle gang that roamed from state to state. He had a wife Barbra Hegel a German woman. She owned a diner in Boulder. Tommy contacts Jim and has him interview Barbra. Around 6pm Jim gets back with Tommy. Barbra was a big brawny rough talking woman. I thought she was going to bite my head off. Jim joked. I am glad you survived did you get anything from her? We did! It turns out Barbra isn't too happy with Big John. Turns out he left her for a younger blonde bimbo as she put it. She told me that he and some of those Wolverine pals of his were holding up at a farmhouse in Indiana. Indiana? Yeah, it's a stretch but she gave me an address and I gave it to your FBI friend Nicole. She is Harvey's sister. Oh, you don't say! YES, I DO. That's something I heard she was somewhere in the middle east. Jim replies. She was but the FBI brought her in to catch these guys and offered her a job. I

bet Harvey is happy. Oh, he is he is right here. Hi Jim. Harvey said. Hey, Harvey, how's that beautiful wife of

yours? She is doing fine. Sam says as she walks in. Oh, hey there Samantha! Jim says as he saw her appear

on the monitor. Anyways have a goodnight if I hear anymore, I will let you know. Thanks, and we will do the

same. They disconnect the video call. It was 6:40 pm. The dogs began whining and barking as they her

Nicole's Lincoln pull in; they close the door and walk upstairs. Oh, hi there, guys. I have Chinese as promised.

Good let's eat. They all sit at the Table. Let's pray. Harvey stands and says. They all bow their heads. Lord, I

thank you for this day and for this food we are about to eat. I ask that you sanctify it and make it good for us

to eat in Jesus' name I pray, amen.

They sit down and begin eating. This
is delicious thanks so much Nicole. Sam
said. Your welcome. So how was you
guys day? It was productive we think we
may have located Big Jim. Yes, thanks I
got the voicemail from Jim on the way
home. Indiana? Wow that's something. I
had a swat team from our field in Indiana.
They are headed there now. After dinner

they head to the living room area. Nicole begins talking with Harvey and Samantha. So, tell me more about how you guys met and all. And what do you do Samantha? I am a schoolteacher for fourth graders. Oh, wow you have it rougher than we do! Nicole says. I doubt that my class don't try to kill me every day. Good point but I rather be shot at than must deal with a bunch a kids. Nicole says. Guess it takes us all to make things work out. Samantha replies. True Samantha it does Harvey adds. So how did you meet? It was when our class took a field trip to Fort Collins and when the gas leak explosion happened. Harvey was my hero during that and when the Truck nearly killed us. So, you guys came together during times of crisis. Yes, we did. But we started talking before then. Oh, I wasn't implying anything and meant no disrespect Samantha. I know I was pointing out we had started semi dating before all this. That's great to hear. I heard you guys got married in Hawaii. We sure did Samantha replied. That is so cool. Nicole replied. How did you make that happen Harvey? I had saved for four years to go there and had planned of going this year. So, when I fell in love with Samantha I just went ahead and made the trip. He purposed to me in front of this mountains waterfall it was so romantic, when I said yes, he had the minister and a wedding party come and we got married. Sam continued. You, ole Casanova you. Nicole punches Harvey in the shoulder. Harvey grins. It was 11pm. Nicole's phone lit up! It's a warzone out here they have got a gatling gun and they are raining fire down us like we have never faced! They have snipers with 50 caliber rifles shooting at us. A couple of our guys have headed their head blown clean off. We need the National guard now are were all dead! I will do what I can as quick as I can try and hang on! Please, hurry! Nicole calls Washington and at 12am there was a F16 Jet and three-gun ship helicopters came. The Jet fired a missile near home destroying half of the house the mercenaries scattered, and the gunships began picking them off. At 1am there was silence. The swat team charges the home carefully in case the place was wired. They reach the home and see a bunker nearby. It was sealed from the outside. The bore a small hole and ran a camera in there, as the camera reached the opening, they could see Big John and a prison cell with about ten girls inside. They had attached a small tranquilizer gun that was controlled by remote on the camera. Once they got big John in its sights they fired. The dart struck him in the back of the neck as he had been back to the camera. He reached and grabs the dart and within seconds he hits the floor. They had hit him with the right amount of tranquilizer it knocked slap out. They quickly blow the door and propel down. They secure the man and release the girls. They radio Nicole and let them know it was done. They send Big John to Captain Stevens in Denver via Chopper and in the morning, Nicole interrogates him, and he gives up the location of Carlos and crew. Nicole video calls Tommy And tells him they found where they are. Do you guys want in? She asked. Yes! Tommy and Harvey say. Sarah says she will sit this one out and stay With Sam. Nicole tells Harvey and Tommy to suit up and she would pick them up in an hour. They grab their gear and their weapons. Be careful Harvey I want my Honey to come home tonight. Sure, thing baby. Harvey kisses her. I love you. I love you too. Sam says as he holds him tight. Sarah hugs Tommy. Go get them tiger she says. I sure will. The dogs bark as if to agreed. An hour later 10am on Thursday September 15 Nicole picks them up. They head out. So, where are they? Kansas. In an underground bunker near Indian lake. They coordinate with local police and with the Kansas City national guard. They find an architect who had built the underground tunnels and the bunker, and he showed them away to get in without being detected. The entrance was under water in the lake. So, they put on their scuba gear and go for a swim. The entrance was a gate that the underwater generator wires were run through. The wires were in large waterproof tubing which left a man-sized hole that they could slip through, but they would have to go one by one. Tommy goes through then Harvey, then Nicole. The team of about thirty seal team members go through next. Once they get past the entrance and enter through the airlock door. They remove their oxygen tanks and masks and send out their miniature drone to scope out the tunnels. They notice in three of the tunnels there were cells of about a 100 cages in each. And there were hundreds maybe more boys and girls in these unsanitary conditions. How were they going to get them to the surface? At each cell block were three guards. Down a piece they spotted ten more guards. Just beyond them were a group of twenty or more. And then beyond that was an

office. Inside the office were Carlos,
Enrique and crew. They had about fifteen
men with them and they were armed to
the gills. Tommy and Harvey secure
tunnel one, Nicole and five of her men
secure the other two. They secure the
prisoners and then the rest of the group
head up and throw gas grenades into the
first wave. They have masks. So, as they
approached the mercenaries, they simply
disarmed them and bound them as they
were knocked out. They do the same to
the rest and just walk up to the office
without making a sound. They surround
the door and crack it open and throw in
more grenades within minutes Carlos and
company were all subdued. There reign
of terror had come to an end. After
finding a map in office of the tunnels the
discover a freight elevator that went to
the top. They inform Captain Stevens of

the location and began sending up the prisoners all of which were under the age of 19. Captain Stevens arrive with ambulance and Fire rescue and the whole army of volunteers. It was a massive operation and many girls and boys were rescued and sent for hospital care and counseling. Many were reunited with their families. It was an eventful day full of joy and celebration by the time they secured the mercenaries and Carlos. It was 8pm. They head home to Nicole's. Harvey dials Samantha. Hi baby. Hey Harvey, it's good to hear your voice. Yours too Sam. I am glad you're okay. How is Tommy and Nicole being all good. We are heading there now. Sarah is hear squealing in the background. We saw the whole thing on the news! You guys did it! Yes, we all did. They hang up and Nicole tells them there welcome to stay if they like. Tommy says he and Sarah would stay the night and head home in the morning. How about you and Sam. I know you will be starting your internship next week and their office is across the street from ours. You guys are welcome to live with me while you do this. Thanks for the offer sis. I will discuss it with Samantha and let you know. It was 12 am by the time they got home and ate and settled in. Harvey presents Nicole's offer to Sam and asks her what she thought. It sounds cool with me my school called and said they were having to layoff folks, so I volunteered to be laid off. There is an opening at Nicole's office for a secretary that pays a lot more than what I made at school. I got the job start next week. That settles it then Nicole says. You guys live here as long as you want to. I am hardly hear and the dogs get lonely, plus I get lonesome when I am here. So, they agree and go to bed. Samantha and Harvey hold one another in bed and fall asleep in the morning Tommy and Sarah say goodbye and they would see them later. Harvey said he would be at work on Monday. Tommy and Sarah said there was no need to work out anymore of his notice as he had done enough. They wished him luck with his new venture. And head home. Harvey and Samantha didn't realize they would never see them again.

Chapter 10

Life after the storm

That Monday, Harvey and Sam decide to do something nice for Nicole. So, they head to town and go grocery shopping and to the local Walmart. They find a nice smart watch and buy it for her. They come home and unload groceries and Samantha cooks them a supper. A chicken parmesan with fettuccine Alfaro and a side salad. For dessert she makes a Butterfinger cheesecake to die for. They clean the house walk the dogs and feed the others. They wait for her to come home. When she arrives, she is surprised! Thanks guys I was expected supper and the house cleaned and the dogs fed! Wow! Your awesome after dinner. This was delicious thanks so much! Hope you saved room for dessert. Dessert? Yes, dessert, Sam said as she brought out the cheesecake. Butterfinger Cheesecake that is my favorite! This is the best cheesecake I have ever eaten. Thanks so much! After dessert Harvey cleans the dishes and the table. They sit in the living room chilling out when Samantha walks up and hands her a bag. What is this? It's just a gift from us to say thanks for being so good to us. Oh, thanks you guys didn't have to do all this. I didn't expect nothing back I did because I love you all. We know but we just wanted to. Let me see what this then. She opens it and it's an apple smart watch.

Nicole laughs with excitement.

This is the exact watch I wanted.

Thanks guys how did you know? I

saw your phone and your wish

list. Harvey said. Nicole laughed.

Come here you two. She give

them a hug and a kiss. This

means so much. I haven't had

anything given to me or done for

me in a long time. Nicole weeps

with joy. She puts it on and

connects it with her iPhone 11. It

is beautiful the white band

matches my phone thanks again.

How was your day? She asked

them. It was nice we went

shopping and it was nice to get

out of the house Samantha said.

So, you start your internship

Next Monday then. She asked

Harvey. Yes, I do. And I start next Monday at your office Sam added. That's cool. So, what are your plans for this week? Not sure guess were open for anything. I have time off for this week too and I thought we could go to Panama City beach Florida together if you would like? We would love too. Great get packed we our plane leaves in two hours. It was 8pm and the flight left for Florida at 10pm. They pack and head out. Upon arriving at the gate, they were directed to gate B32 and when they arrived the stewardess took their tickets. First Class to the left. First Class? Harvey and Sam were amazed. They walk up front and find their seats the seats were soft leather with higher backs and more space. The food choices were better and of course they had an assortment of acholic drinks. Which was not appealing to them. But they did enjoy the sodas. It was a pleasant ride and Nicole was in the seat an isle across. They arrive at the airport at Panama City it was 1am they grab their bags and are driven to Edgewater Hotel where Nicole had adjoining room next to theirs. They settle in and walk out on the patio and watch the waves crash on the beach. This is so nice! Samantha said as she held his hand. Nicole knocked. You guys like your room? Yes, we do. Is yours nice? Yes, it is. I leave you two lovebirds alone I'm going to get some sleep.

Samantha grabs Harvey by the

hand and whispers in his ear.

Make love to me.

He kisses her lips softly as the lie on the bed and turn

out the light. In the morning

they wake up Nicole is in her

bathing suit. You guys coming?

Yes, we are. Samantha throws

on hers and Harvey puts on his

swim shorts. And they head out

on the beach. It was a lot of fun

that week that laughed and

played and really got to know his

sister. Saturday, they fly home

and rest the weekend for

Monday. Sunday Harvey and

Sam get ready for church they

invite Nicole she agrees, and

they go to church together.

There greeted with smiles, hugs

and handshakes. Harvey and Nicole were honored for their part in the major arrests of those evil men. The sermon was on love thy neighbor. After church they were all chatting and a tall dark handsome man in his forties approached Nicole. Hi I am David. He says as he holds out his hand. I'm Nicole as she hands out hers. I don't mean to be too direct, but you are beautiful. Nicole blushes. I was wondering if perhaps I could take you to dinner sometime. She looked surprised. Yes, I wouldn't mind. I have a busy schedule how about tonight. That's great want to meet at 8. Yes, I will meet you here at the church. It's a date then. David says see you then.

Samantha came to Nicole. He is handsome Nicole what did he want? To take me to dinner. Wow! That is awesome! You will be happy when you get to know him. How so? He is a lot of fun and he is rich. He started his own software security business and has made millions. He is the most desirable bachelor on the market these days. Nicole raised an eyebrow. Have fun tonight. We will hold down the fort at home. Okay let's go home then. They get home and Harley walks the dogs and feeds them. Nicole gets ready fixes her hair puts on makeup and puts on this shiny red dress. Wow! You look hot! Sam said. Oh, please! Nicole said blushing. At 7 she heads back to the church. She arrives at the church at 7:45 and David is already there. In brand new blue Nissan Altima. She gets out he greets her and opens the door to his Altima. The seats were leather with heat adjustments there was a nice touchscreen radio with GPS and a backup camera with Alexa voice activated calling. I hope you like Mediterranean and Mexican Cuisine. Love it cannot wait. Where are we going? To El Five restaurant I already decided for an outdoor private area. That's nice cannot wait. They arrive and are seated and talk until their food comes. So, you're into Software Security? Yes, its actual

Cybersecurity but that's what I call my company product.

I hear you are an FBI agent. That's right. Aren't you the one who busted that sex traffic ring? Well, I was the agent who directed it. But it was a major collaboration of law enforcement that made it happen. I must say you look ravishing tonight. Thanks, and you look nice to David. He grins. Their food arrives and they finish. David takes her to a Sympathy, and they have a wonderful evening. He takes her back to the church at 11pm. He holds open the door and help her out. Nicole gives him her number. Call me sometime if you want to. I sure would I would like to take you out for a night on the town again. I would like that too. He shakes her hand and Nicole kisses him on the cheek. He opens her car door and says goodbye. Nicole felt alive for the first time in years. She was as giddy as a teenager. She drives home and Harvey and Sam were watching TV. Hi guys she said with excitement. I take the date went good Sam said. Yes, you can say that he is wonderful. I feel like a teenager again. Samantha grins Harvey was passed out asleep. Nicole and Sam sit up until two in the morning talking girl talk. They finally must go to bed as Sam starts her new job today. She snuggles on the couch and falls asleep on Harvey's lap. 6am

came fast Nicole is heard
grunting and stretching and then
hoping in the shower. Sam and
Harvey awaken and get ready.
Harvey had to be at the law
office at 10, Sam and Nicole had
to be at their office at 9. So, they
got ready and Nicole and Sam
left for work. Harvey had
sometime so he calls Tommy.
There was no answer. He calls
Sarah no answer. It worried him
but he went on to work and had
his first day at work. It went well
the lawyers and staff were
genuinely nice. He was famous
because of the arrests.
Samantha has a great day but a
busy one. Nicole got some sad
news.

Chapter 11

Tragic news!

Nicole couldn't tell Harvey or Sam until they all got
home. Time came for Nicole and
Samantha to get off the work.
Nicole walks to Samantha.
Ready to go? Yes, let's go. How
was your first day? It was good.
Very busy but I like it. That's
good to hear. Nicole was somber
on the way home it was mostly
silent. Sam knew something
wasn't right, but she didn't want
to pry. They arrive at home.
Harvey arrives minutes later.
Guys come sit I have something
to tell you. What is it? Harvey
asked. Well its Tommy and
Sarah. What about them?
Samantha asked. We just got

news there was another accident in the Fort Collins area. They found Tommy's SUV Crushed under a rock that fell from the mountain. Was Tommy? Sarah? No, they were not found. But the worst an avalanche wiped out their home. It's under a pile of rocks. How? What happened? It seems that someone had stolen Tommy's jeep the same time the avalanche happened. Because there was an unknown male found in the Bronco. But we don't know if Sarah are Tommy were home or not. We have no way of knowing until the debris is cleared. I want to help. Harvey said. I don't think that would be good Harvey Sam said. I know honey it's just not knowing what happened to them is hard to deal with. We're doing everything we can. In fact, we have ordered an evacuation of the town. Do you think everyone will abide by this? No, but we have blocked all entry levels to the town. Whoever doesn't leave will be on their own. We believe it's way too dangerous to allow this town to continue to be occupied. I pray Sarah and Tommy are okay, but I fear the worst, because it all happened at night when would have been asleep. When this happen? Just last night. That explains why I couldn't reach them this morning. Harvey was worried So was Samantha. Nicole was too Sarah was her friend. She looked at her phone for the first time since getting

home. There was a missed call

from David. She sent him a text

explaining the situation and

apologized that she was way too

busy at this time. He replied

sorry to hear I pray they are

okay. Tell Samantha and Harvey

they are in my prayers as you

are, too. Thanks David perhaps

in a week or two we can go out

but for now she had to

concentrate on her work. They

go to bed Harvey moaned and

cried out through the night.

Morning came and it was off to

work. Samantha and Nicole

leave first. Harvey stays behind.

He prays and prays some more.

He decides to call the law office

and let them know he wasn't

coming in. he wasn't getting paid anyhow. They thanked him for calling and hoped to see him on the morrow. He agreed grabbed his deputy Marshall uniform and gun and head to Fort Collins. He arrives and flashes his badge and they let him pass. He drives to Tommy and Sarah's home or what was left of it. He knew something that the others didn't know. Tommy had an underground bunker and a hidden entrance. He slips behind the house to find the entrance it was still intact and hadn't been crushed under the rocks. He opens the door and enters, checking the steadiness of the bunker it seemed intact. He proceeded deeper into the bunker. And hidden in the back corner was a camera and monitor. He turned it on. It was Tommy if anyone sees this. The Avalanche was caused by the mercenaries. There were still a sect left and they sat off explosions. Sarah and I have left the town and have relocated. The film stopped. He searched and found another video it read: To Harley and Samantha Coles and To Nicole. He plays it and, in its Tommy, explains when they said goodbye that morning they left for Hawaii and were living in Honolulu. And not to worry. There is a safe deposit box in the Bank of OZK in Denver and the keys are in this desk drawer. We want you all to have what's in it.

And Harvey we are alive and well
enjoy your new life with your
wife and sister. And do not look
for us as we can have no contact
with anyone ever. They had been
placed in witness protection as
they had put away those men
they were being hunted. Harvey
you and Sam will be safe living
with Nicole. So, don't worry
about us we will be fine. Sarah
sends her love and we wish you
all the best. Then video ended.
Harvey felt relieved they were
not in this rubble that was once
their home. They never came
home he checked the desk on so
ticket receipts to Hawaii for day
they left. He breathed a sigh of
relief and he took the videos and
went to his car and drove back

home. On the way he called Sam and told her what he found. That's great news! I know your relieved. I am. I know I shouldn't have gone without telling you or Nicole. But I knew you would resist. But I had to go because I knew of the bunker and no one else did. I understand honey I am not upset I am so glad you found out where they were.

I will see you at home okay sweetie stay safe. Always baby, always. Sam laughed and hung up. He calls Nicole and tells her. Good work Harvey that saved us form digging through piles of rock. I know should have told you. Nah, you shouldn't because It would have taken an act of congress and the window of opportunity may have slipped away. Alright then I will see you

at home. Harvey goes to the

bank and finds the box and

opens it. Inside was 20 million

dollars! Harvey nearly fainted.

Also, inside was Tommy's Civil

War relics worth over 100,000.

He puts the relics in the baggie

he had brought and the cash too.

He puts the box back and heads

to the car. He drives home and

waits for Sam and Nicole. When

they arrive, he gathers them at

the table and tells them the

whole story. He explains that the

contents of the box belonged to

them. What was in there? They

asked. He puts the bag on the

table and dumps it out. 20

million dollars! How did it

happen, they had this much? I

don't know but it is here. Well, what do you plan on doing? Well, I thought I would ask you guys. Well, it was to all of us, so let's pray about this. I think we should give ten percent to the church. I agree. Harvey said to Sam. Nicole thought that would be good too. How much you owe on the house and the car? Oh, I am not sure exactly but you sure you want to this? Of course, you're my sister and you have been so good to me and Sam. Samantha agreed. So, she gave him the car balance and the house mortgage balance. It added up to 250,000 all together as she had paid on the mortgage and the car for about 3 years. So, in the morning Nicole calls the mortgage company and pays off the house and the car. It felt so good to do she felt like a heavy burden had been lifted she had called in and so had Sam. They put two million in an envelope and mail it to the church. Harvey and Sam go shopping they buy clothes and a couple of computer tablets and smartwatches. Harvey goes to an Academy store and buys some fishing gear. He also buys stock in Amazon and opens a savings account. He buys a 40-caliber handgun and an AR15. Nicole goes and makes plans to tour Ireland, Australia and to Hawaii again. She had discussed this with them the night before. They send a cash donation to homeless shelter building project. They helped rescue

animals and shut down a local kill

shelter. They donated ten

thousand to the women shelters

who helped rescue women. At

5pm the three of them met at

home and told of all they did.

Harvey showed his guns to his

sister. Those are nice that 40

Smith and Wesson is a sweet

shooter. The AR is a nice rifle for

hunting or if you get into a major

gun fight. Samantha showed her

the clothes and her tablet and

smartwatch and new phone.

Nicole showed them the deed

and title to her car. It was a fun

night. So how much is left? 15

million. That's good we will have

a lot of fun on our three-trip tour.

They go to bed and on

Wednesday morning they are at the airport heading to Ireland. They would spend a week in Ireland then they would visit Israel as a bonus for a week. The view the empty tomb the wailing wall and all the land Jesus walked. While in Israel they helped feed and house hundreds of holocaust survivors. While there they gave a donation to local missionaries then went to Australia. They only spent three days there as they spent 14 in Israel and Ireland. They buy lots of souvenirs and then they flew to Hawaii. They spent a week there and enjoyed the beach and mountains before returning home. They arrive home two months later. Harvey had acquired the credentials need to take the bar. He had taken it before leaving. The mailbox was overflowing, and packages were at the door. Harvey picks up the packages and the mail and brings it in the house. Samantha and Nicole had begun unloading the car. Harvey comes out and helps them within a few minutes they had it unloaded the car and had crashed on the couch. What was in those boxes? I don't know they were addressed to all of us. No return address. Well let's see what it is. Harvey grabs them and slowly opens it. Inside was a picture of Tommy and Sarah from where they were that read Hello, we miss you guys.

They hang the picture on the wall, then open the others. One was a plaque with a Bible verse. PSALMS 23. The last one was a family Bible with pictures of Harvey and Nicole in them as children and of their mom. They spent the night looking at the photos well into the night. It was Saturday night in the morning the all went to church. At the service, the pastor revealed the 2-million-dollar tithe gift in the mail the other day. He prayed that God would bless the secret tither in a mighty way. The money given and David's weekly tithe helped open a 7day soup kitchen and a homeless shelter that they ran 7 days a week. A much-needed ministry made possible by the gifts of David and Harvey, Sam and Nicole. But only David was known to the church who tithed that much or more every week.

After the service David approached Nicole and spoke to her. He asked her and Harvey and Sam to dinner. They agreed and then Sam and Harvey went home and left them there alone. David and Nicole spent the day together. She and he agree to see each other again.

Harvey and Samantha spent the time to be together and to relax. The next day Samantha and Nicole return to work after a two-month hiatus. It was a rough day of returning to work physically and mentally getting used to the grind. Harvey takes an account of the amount left

6million remained in cash 2
million in savings and he had
passed the bar, so he went and
got his business and license to
become a lawyer. He purchased
an older house in town paying
cash paying 200,000 and got the
deed and bought office furniture
and hired a receptionist. And
began practicing law. As soon as
he opened, he had a handful of
people that wanted help filing for
disability filing a lawsuit against
the city and so on a so forth.
Then before closing a man walks
in. He was a hairy man a
homeless man. Who had been
accused of murder? Harvey could
not believe the man could hardly
walk let alone kill anyone. He
contacted Stevens and got the

police report. He promised the man he would help him. I can't pay much. No need to pay me at all. Where can I reach you. At the shelter. Okay give me three days and I will come find you Mr. Daniels. You can call me Leon the man said as he staggered away. Harvey closes and locks the door and heads home. He arrives home an hour before Nicole and Sam do. He orders two pizzas and some cheesy sticks and a brownie. And has it delivered the delivery man arrives thirty minutes later. Harvey gives the driver a thirty - dollar tip. The driver thanked him and was shocked. The driver left and Harvey brought the pizzas and put them on the table.

He hears Nicole's Lincoln in the drive and hears them he sits in the living room and waits. Oh, what a tiring day. Sam says. Your telling me and now we got to.... What? Pizza! Yes! Surprise! Harvey says. Samantha grabs him and kisses him. Thanks, so much baby it means so much to me. Yes, thanks so much. Nicole says as she sits and grabs a slice then looks at Harvey. You going to ask God to bless it so we can eat. Yes, for sure. Lord, thanks so much for your blessings and for this food. Amen. Thanks, let's eat. Nicole takes a bite and relishes it. Sam sits and Harvey and they eat. After dinner they ask what Harvey was up to today. Glad you asked. I opened a law office. I already have five clients. One of which I am not charging for. Because he is homeless. I hired a receptionist and bought a townhouse for my practice. Congratulations bro! you made it happen. Yes baby, that is awesome. We wish you the best. Only I need to meet your receptionist and see what she looks like. Okay you can meet her tomorrow if you can come by at lunch. Alright I will you got a lunch date. Looking forward to it. They spend the night watching a movie and go to bed the next day they go to work before Samantha leaves, she reminds him of their lunchtime appointment. Harvey follows up on his cases and sets an appointment with the arresting officer. He would meet him at his office at 5pm. At 12pm sharp Samantha walks in as well as Nicole. And Judy, the receptionist greets them. She was a 65-year-old lady. Nicole and Sam look at each other and grin. Are you ready Harvey asked? Yes, were going to buffaloes steak house. Want to come Judy? Samantha asked. Sure, Judy said. The four of them walk out and Harvey locks the door. They drive to the restaurant and Harvey introduces Judy to Samantha and Nicole. They get to know Judy a widow and a longtime resident of Denver town. Her husband was an oil rig worker and he provided for her and their two children May and Max. One day there was an explosion the rig and he was killed leaving me to fend for myself and two kids. I went to work in a doctor's office for years until the doctor retired. She raised her kids and was now living alone and needed some extra money to live. After lunch they return to Harvey's office and Sam kisses Harvey and says goodbye. Nicole says they would see him later and   wished Judy well.

Harvey went to work in the office and told Judy when officer jones arrived to send him in. He arrives and Judy sends him in. Harvey interviews him and finds that his client was seen leaving the scene where the victim's body was. Did you find the weapon? Yes, a sledgehammer. The man was beat to death, have you paid attention to the guy you arrested? Not really, I just arrived on the scene and figured it was him. So, you assumed he did it? Yeah, I mean no. which is it you did or didn't? Look it was my first arrest I didn't pay attention to the man. So, you saw a man near the scene and assumed he was the perp and arrested a 75-year-old 120 man. He didn't even give you no trouble arresting him, did he? No, he didn't! He seemed too frail to have done it come to think of it. Thank you, I think you should make an apology to my client and tell your captain you made a mistake. I thank you for your time. I will be in touch if I need more. Thank you please don't get me fired. I'm not you just pray they don't fire you once a lawsuit is filed for false arrest. Once he left, he presented his case and played the recording of the policeman's interview. The district attorney agreed to drop the charges and apologize to the man. Harvey asks Judy to contact the city homeless shelter. She does and asks for Mister Daniels. Oh, you mean Jimmy. Wait a sec I will go fetch him. Jimmy! What is it? It's your lawyer on the phone. Oh, let me have It then. Hello, Yes Mr. Daniels this is Judy with Harvey's law office we have good news!

You do? Yes sir, the charges have been dropped you have been cleared. That's awesome! I am so happy! Yes sir, also the police officer and the DA will be apologizing to you. Thanks so much. I am so sorry I cannot pay. You don't owe us nothing sir it was totally free for you. Thanks for using Harvey's law office. Your welcome. If you ever need us for anything just call us or stop by. Thanks, I will, and I will tell my friends. Thanks, stay warm tonight. Will do. Harvey had a thought the homeless shelter needs some improvements he contacted a contractor and got some quotes. It was time to go home so Harvey and Judy close shop. Good work on the win

Harvey that was so awesome!
See you in the morning. Alright
stay warm. Sure thing. Harvey
drives home. It was 7pm by the
time he got home he had stayed
late settling the case. At home
Nicole and Samantha were
already home. Nicole had on a
blue dress and was all dolled up.
You going somewhere? Harvey
asked. Yes, David and I are going
to a symphony. Don't stay up for
my dad, it will be late. She
jested. Before you go, I settled
my first case and it was out of
court! Awesome bro give me
five. Nicole slaps his hand.
Samantha congratulates him
with a hug and a kiss. Weeks go
by and Harvey's practice gains a
lot of fame, so much so he had to

hire in another lawyer. His
business did so well because he
fought for the underdog. He also
had the shelter improved with
central heating and air and six
bathrooms with actual cubicle
rooms for each one to sleep in.
He had all new mattresses put in
and TVS and made the shelter
more like a home. Harvey was
the hero for the homeless. He
won several disability cases too
and made a lot of money
defending and suing for others.
David and Nicole became very
close and one day David
purposed. Nicole accepted and
they were married in the church.
On a Sunday afternoon. They
honeymooned in Paris France.
Nicole moved in with David and

wrote Harvey and Samantha the deed to the house since he had paid for it. Harvey buys Sam a Dodge Charger and he buys him a Chevy HD Extended cab truck. There life was complete. David and Nicole took cruises and had house in Georgia and Tennessee they also had a Condo in Florida. They did anything and everything they wanted they helped fed people gave the homeless homes and helped in church missions. Harvey fought for the rights of Christians and Samantha kept working with the FBI office.

Chapter 12

The stones fall.

On a   Monday in December the air was bitter *cold*. A

dark grey sky hung over the sky. Nicole calls Harvey to see how he was. I am good and you? I am good

working on a case in Fort Collins. Saw Sam this morning and she said to tell you she loved you and she would

see you tonight. By the way david and I are coming over for dinner tonight. You, are? Great it will be nice to

see you again it's been a couple of months. Yes, I know we all have been busy. You have an actual law firm

now and doing so much good for the community and Sam has been busy at work also. We finally settled

down and got back to work now. What's going on in Fort Collins. Someone has been messing around the

town and in and out of the abandoned houses. Mostly squatters and thugs. But it seems to be operation

coming out of the town. We had blocked the entryways to the town and posted no trespassing signs. But

that did not stop the vagrants. But it has more than vagrants. There has been a lot of Heroin being sold out

of here. So, were trying to ascertain the location of the distribution. I think I can give you a location. Where?

Well, they had been making heroin in an abandoned coal mine. Just up the mountain. We thought that we

had shut it down, but it appears they may be using it again. Thanks Harvey I will check into it. Be careful you

really should call for back up. I know brother, but it will be fine I have my pits with me. Oh, you still got them

dogs yes, and they are quite the protectors. I bet they are. Please call me when you get through, I want rest

until I know you're okay. I will Harvey take care and I will see you guys at dinner. I hear Sam is cooking Nola

BBQ shrimp. Sounds good, that girl sure can cook. You got you a good woman. Oh, you don't have to tell me

I know. Alright Harv, I let you get back to lawyering and I will get to checking out this lab. And if it makes you

feel better, I have called it in. Good to know sis, good to know. Bye. Harvey hangs up. As soon as he does a

pastor walks in. Yes, may I help you? Yes, Harvey, I believe you can. It seems they are trying to build a bar on our property we own next door to us. Now we have the deeds to the land, and we do not want a bar next to our church where kids play, and the parishioners would think we condoned drinking. I am sorry I didn't catch your name. Oh, I apologize, I am Brother John Hopkins pastor of New faith Baptist Church. Do you have the deeds with you? Yes, I do in fact. Here they are. Harvey looks them over and sees they are all correct and intact. It seems we have a slam dunk case Pastor Hopkins. That's good to hear son. How much will we owe you? There will be no charge for my services if you tell me why New faith? Well, the church used to be ran by and worshipped in satan worshippers. Harvey's eyes got big! You bought a church where they worshipped the devil? Not exactly we tore that building down and poured slab and built a new church hence the name New faith. That sure is something. I mean to go from a devil worshipping area to a house of the Lord. No wonders the bar thinks it can build there then. We will put a stop to this by the afternoon. Thanks, so much Harvey. You're a good man. I appreciate that but there is none good save the Lord. You are right there Harvey. Pastor Hopkins says as he leaves. Harvey gets on the phone to the building permit office. And explains the issue with the bar. We see that the property is owned by the church and we will deny them access to this lot or any lot in that vicinity as it is owned by the church and a school owns the other. Thanks for bringing this to our attention. Judy can you call Pastor Hopkins and tell him the issue has been resolved. Sure, thing boss, you know I hate it when you call me that. I know I just like to yank your chain. I know Judy and I appreciate the humor. At 5pm it was time to go home so he leaves the firm to his other lawyers to handle. And he goes home night Judy Night Harvey. Harvey gets in his pickup and calls Sam. You need anything before I get home baby. Some more sodas would be good and some cream cheese for my cheesecake. Got it. Thanks sweetie you're the best. No babe you are. Harvey hangs up and the phone rings. Hello hey bro, I checked out your tip and sure enough there is something going down there, and it appears the squatters have taken up permanent residence there. It doesn't surprise me now that Tommy and Sarah

aren't there. Don't forget you too. You guys together kept that place free of crimes for the most part. We did

our best until Carlos and our dad came to town. I am on my way home; Sam is cooking and wants me to pick

up some drinks. What does David like? He loves DR. Pepper it's his favorite. Alright he's my kind of guy that

is mine too. See you guys at 7? For sure we will be there. See you. Harvey pulls into the store and buys four

12 packs of Dr. Pepper and 3 packs of Pepsi Sam's favorite. Nicole liked Dr. Pepper too, so he got one more

pack of pepper and Pepsi. He grabs the Philadelphia cream cheese and goes to the register. Pays the cashier

and walks out and puts it in the car. As he backs out, he hears sirens and a helicopter flying over. He

wondered what was going on. But he headed home. He pulls in and Samantha meets him at the car with a

kiss and helps him bring in the drinks and the cream cheese. Thanks sweetie. She runs to kitchen and

finishes her cheesecake. She comes out and straitens her hair and runs to the bedroom to change. Harvey

freshens up and the doorbell rings. Harvey opens the door and David and Nicole come in. Samantha comes

out in a brown skirt with a white blouse she was beautiful with her hair up in a comb. Harvey compliments

her and so does Nicole and David. It smells so good Sam and love how you have decorated the house and

made it yours. Harvey helps Sam sit the table. Harvey asks the blessing on the food and they begin eating.

This is delicious Sam. David replied. Yes, it is you should open your own restaurant your so talented at

cooking. Nicole tells her. Thanks, it's my passion I love to cook and bake. I think you would enjoy running a

restaurant for real. Yeah, I have dreamed of it, but I wouldn't want the hassle of running it I would just want

to cook and bake. What if I told you, I could make that happen? I would probably jump at the chance to do

the thing I love every day. Well, this is one reason we came tonight. I have bought a restaurant downtown

and I was looking for a head chef and co-owner of the restaurant. Sign me up David. When can I start?

Tomorrow would be good. Its Saturday and you could check it out before making your final decision. But as co=owner you will receive half the profits and a bonus for being the chef. That's an awesome offer. I can't wait to see it tomorrow. Was there another reason? Yes, we wanted to tell you guys, were pregnant! Congratulations that is awesome. I know it is Nicole smiles. Yes, congratulations Nicole that is so awesome. That's why we wanted to tell you guys first so we could celebrate it tonight. Here is dessert. Sam says carrying her famous cheesecake. After dinner Harvey asked if Nicole knew what was up with the sirens and the choppers. Well, they raided the heroin lab and there was a bit of a standoff, so they called in reinforcements. They were able to capture and destroy and seal of that mine completely so that no more labs would be made there. The town was full of spectators. The squatters I imagine. They said there were hundreds of them. They didn't concern themselves with them as they presented no threat. But Captain Stevens said he would round them up and put up a ten-foot fence to keep anyone from getting in. that's the latest anyways. David and Nicole hung out for a while as they played some cards and charades. David was a lot of fun quite the funny guy. They decide to leave as it was getting late. David said he would see Samantha tomorrow and hoped they had a goodnight. Sam and Harvey cleaned up the mess and sat on the couch, the kissed and held one another. And went to bed kissing and holding one another. They hadn't gone asleep when they heard more helicopters and more ambulances. Something was up. Harvey turns on the news. There was major landslide tonight in in the town of Fort Collins the rocks slides were so intense it has buried the town in which Marshalls tommy and Sarah took much care and keeping it safe. They left months ago but now town is reduced the rubble there have been reports of hundreds of squatters living in the homes are now buried underneath a rocky grave. We will have more on this story at the 6 am news. Wow! It happed the rocks fell and destroyed he town just as they did in the upper valley town. It's a shame those folk were killed but it is good news that no one else will have to die in that town. A history of death and sorrows were associated with those two towns and now the saga had ended. The stones all came down. Samantha grabs Harvey's hand. I have some news of my own. What is it? WE Are Pregnant!

The End!

Made in the USA
Columbia, SC
11 September 2023